Brain Games

SHARON HAMBRICK

JOURNEYFORTH

Greenville, South Carolina

Hambrick, Sharon, 1961
    Brain games / Sharon Hambrick.
        p. cm.
    Summary: Whether facing the challenges of assembling a team of
academically gifted students for the statewide Superbrains competition
or battling cancer, Judson Christian High School's favorite teacher,
Miss Thistle, depends on the Lord Jesus.
    ISBN 978 1 59166 954 8 (perfect bound pbk. : alk. paper)
    [1. Teachers—Fiction. 2. High schools—Fiction. 3. Schools—Fiction.
4. Contests—Fiction. 5. Christian life—Fiction.] I. Title.
    PZ7.H1755Br 2009
    [Fic]—dc22

                                                                2008049163

Cover Photos: Craig Oesterling/(hand); www.istockphoto.com/Stefan Klien/
(service bell)

Design by Nathan Hutcheson
Page layout by Kelley Moore

© 2009 by BJU Press
Greenville, SC 29614
JourneyForth Books is a division of BJU Press

ISBN 978-1-59166-954-8

15   14   13   12   11   10   9   8   7   6   5   4   3   2   1

For Gracie, Meredith, Bethany, and Amanda,
because we had so much fun in our class

Contents

Chapter 1	1
Chapter 2	6
Chapter 3	10
Chapter 4	17
Chapter 5	24
Chapter 6	28
Chapter 7	31
Chapter 8	37
Chapter 9	42
Chapter 10	48
Chapter 11	55
Chapter 12	61
Chapter 13	64
Chapter 14	67
Chapter 15	72
Chapter 16	77
Chapter 17	81
Chapter 18	86
Chapter 19	90
Chapter 20	92
Chapter 21	100
Chapter 22	102
Chapter 23	105
Chapter 24	108
Chapter 25	114
Chapter 26	120

Chapter 1

Miss Maggie Thistle stared at the light blue Superbrains registration form that lay on her desk. Never before in her forty-one years of teaching had it been more important for her that Judson Christian High School field a winning team in the contest. Never before had not one single student applied for the team.

Her eyes drifted over to her gray metal filing cabinet. An old photograph of her parents was held onto the side of the cabinet by a ladybug magnet a student had given her for Christmas years ago. The deep brown face of her father, Homer Thistle, stared back at her from the photo. His hand rested on the shoulder of Minnie Thistle, Miss Thistle's mother and closest confidante, who had spent the summers of her childhood working on a sharecropper's farm.

Miss Thistle touched the photo. How she wished her parents were still living. She wished she could have their advice.

"Ridiculous for a woman my age to need advice!" she said aloud. Then, "If only Sterling hadn't bragged about our kids so!"

Miss Thistle doodled hearts and flowers in the margins of her desk calendar while her mind raced back to that January day two weeks before when Judson Christian had hosted the local principals for the monthly principals' lunch. She had given a short speech on the history of the Superbrains contest, highlighting its importance to the high schools.

Her heart had dropped to her toes when after her talk, Sterling said, "I could pick five Judson kids at random and beat any team any of you could field!"

Challenged, he admitted he'd been kidding and that, no, Judson hadn't done very well at all in recent years, and that it would be hard for any Christian school team in any year to beat any of the teams fielded by the larger, better-funded public schools. In fact, Judson hadn't won since the early sixties.

"My team," Miss Thistle said to herself, remembering the flush of victory when she herself had been the student captain of the team. They'd taken home the state trophy that year—the same trophy that was tarnished and barely noticeable now among the jumble of football, baseball, track, tennis, and marching-band trophies.

It had been a grand moment when, at seventeen, she'd accepted the state Superbrains trophy for Judson Christian. And now in her final year teaching at her alma mater, nothing would please her more than to win it again.

Miss Thistle tapped her pencil on her desk absently for a few minutes, then scooted her chair back and headed out the door for morning teacher devotions. Students and staff called out morning greetings to her as she made her way through them to the office to grab a cup of coffee and get her mail before prayer meeting.

"Are there any prayer requests?" Dr. Sterling Hamilton, the tall, distinguished principal, asked while opening the morning teachers' meeting. He gave the first request himself. "Let's remember Coach Brock and Mrs. Brock at this hard time." A few murmured *amens* floated around the room, echoing Principal Hamilton's feelings. Coach and his wife had been on the way to the hospital to pick up a newborn baby when the birth mother had changed her mind about placing the infant for adoption. The social worker met them at the hospital entrance with pursed lips, shaking her head. "Sorry" was all she needed to say.

Other prayer requests were given: for the student body to follow Christ, for the athletes to display good sportsmanship at the week's events.

Miss Thistle raised her hand. "I have a praise," she said when she was called on. "I want to thank the Lord Jesus for giving me all these years at Judson." She smiled and nodded at the assembled teachers. "And would you please pray about the Superbrains assembly today?"

"Of course," Principal Hamilton said, jotting in his notebook for a moment before asking a few of the teachers to pray.

One teacher he did not call on was Miss Bethany Shore, a third-year government and economics teacher with beautiful long blond hair. Miss Thistle admired Bethany for her ability to walk in three-inch heels and always look flawlessly dressed.

On the other hand, Miss Thistle, with the hindsight of four decades in education, thought it was almost always a mistake to take a young teacher freshly graduated from college and place her in classes of juniors and seniors. The age difference was so small, almost insignificant, and could lead to complications, mostly when newly minted teachers tried too hard to form friendships with students who were closer to their age than the older teachers were.

Miss Shore had a different problem. Instead of wanting the students to like her as a friend, she'd focused on wanting the faculty to accept her as an expert in the field of education.

Miss Thistle sipped her coffee and made a note in her new prayer journal to pray for Miss Shore daily. *Bethany S.: sweet and quiet spirit* was what she wrote.

She called it her new prayer journal, though it was several years old. She'd purchased it in honor of the new millennium on January 2, 2001, having refused throughout the year known as Y2K to acknowledge that the twenty-first century had begun. "The old century does not end until the thousand years have fully elapsed," she told a fair number of people that year. Young people were not always careful about things like that.

Her old prayer journal had fallen apart a number of times, ancient as it was. It was taped and retaped, and now lay in a box on the floor in the back of her closet, behind a number of things she would have thrown out years ago had she been less sentimental.

She made notes of the day's prayer requests and announcements and said good morning to as many of the teachers as she could, though most flooded out into the hall the moment Dr. Hamilton concluded the meeting. Young teachers were often in a hurry to get going. Then again, they still had the ability to rush, whereas she herself was dragged down by a weighty fatigue that nothing had helped. She'd tried food supplements, vitamins, exercise, even a "miracle working powder" she had purchased off a late-night television infomercial. As a last resort, she had visited her general practitioner, Dr. Preston Phillips, himself a Judson grad.

"That follow-up appointment with Preston is today, isn't it, Miss Thistle?" Dr. Hamilton asked kindly when the last staff member had left the room.

"Oh, yes," she replied. "I'm looking forward to hearing what the good doctor prescribes for this fatigue. I guess I shouldn't expect youthful vigor, should I, Dr. Hamilton?"

"Please, Miss Thistle, call me Sterling!" Dr. Hamilton looked down from his six-foot two inches to the five-foot tall woman.

"Of course, Sterling," Miss Thistle laughed. "I just love the sound of that word: Doctor. It carries such achievement, such amazing effort. But of course, you are right. I do remember watching you in after-school detention during the seventies, so I don't always have to be formal, do I?"

"You certainly don't, Miss Thistle," Dr. Hamilton said.

"Call me Maggie," she tossed over her shoulder.

Ninth-grade geography slipped by quickly, and though Miss Thistle was ashamed at how often she yawned during the lesson, she was almost certain the students wouldn't notice. The ninth graders, after all, hadn't known her very long, just up from the junior high school as they were. No doubt they assumed she always yawned her way through classes.

Second hour with eleventh-grade study hall was easier for her physically, as it required no lesson to be presented and gave her time to think about the Superbrains assembly. Her mind wandered, however, and she thought about how Judson Christian High had sprung up in the late sixties as local Christian parents had sought an alternative from the mayhem that seemed to exist on so many campuses during that tense time. Her own parents had sent her there, at enormous financial sacrifice, and she had thrived in the stricter environment. After a two-year stint at the local junior college, she'd come back to teach and had left only once, for one semester, a very long time ago.

It seemed strange to her high school friends when they met at reunions that she had never left. Some of them had lived all over the world and done great things, while she herself had spent year after year in class, in teachers' meetings, in parent-teacher conferences.

"Don't you want to see the world?" a friend had once asked, but she had only shaken her head and said, "I have all the world I need right here."

Someone began coughing, which startled Miss Thistle back to the present. She looked up to see eleventh grader Tim Barnaby with his hand covering his mouth and his whole body shaking with coughs.

"Go get a drink, Tim," Miss Thistle said. Then she frankly stared at the remaining students wondering why their parents allowed them to waste an hour in study hall instead of taking advantage of another math or science course. High school was so short—only four years—and then college, and if you weren't prepared, particularly in math and science, there were so many college majors you simply weren't qualified to pursue.

Take Tim Barnaby for instance. He'd slunk back into his seat in the back row, wiping his mouth and clearing his throat. Miss Thistle was fairly certain Tim was only pretending to read the American History book that lay open on his desk. She knew his type: smart but unmotivated. Tim was the kind of student of whom it was said that he didn't *apply* himself, meaning that he didn't try very hard and only did what was required to secure a respectable grade. There was no drive there, no aspiration for anything more than getting by.

She sighed. "Reminds me of Thaddeus." she said aloud.

"Did you say something, Miss Thistle?" a student asked.

"Yes, but never mind," Miss Thistle said. "My mind was wandering decades back. So sorry."

She had third hour off. She spent the hour tapping her pencil on her desk, rummaging around in her brain for an idea on how to put together a team of Superbrains with an applicant pool of zero. Up until yesterday afternoon, she'd held out hope that someone might apply at the last second, but no one had. She should have informed Dr. Hamilton immediately, of course, but hadn't, for no good reason she could think of.

She stayed at her desk until exactly eleven o'clock, then left for the doctor's office to get those test results.

Chapter 2

The drive wasn't long, and with gas prices what they were, Miss Thistle was relieved once again that she lived in a small town with everything close by. There was still a Main Street with thriving businesses, mostly clothing boutiques and places to eat. Everyone, including herself, did their main grocery shopping at the big-box store outside the city limits. How could you not shop there when prices went up all the time and her salary didn't?

Not that she minded the pay. God had always taken care of her, and besides, her needs were small. Having inherited her parents' home when the Lord took them both to Glory ten years back, she had no mortgage. She hardly ever needed to buy new clothes since she'd been making and mending clothes since she was eleven or twelve when Mama had carefully instructed her in all the domestic skills.

She greeted the receptionist and was quickly ushered into Preston Phillips's book-lined private office. She admired the Doctor of Medicine diploma granted by Johns Hopkins University, her heart beating with personal achievement that a student of hers had excelled so well at such a prestigious school.

Miss Thistle smoothed down her skirt, then folded her hands in her lap. She cleared her throat. She swallowed. "Well, Dr. Phillips, what's the verdict?"

When he answered her, she bowed her head over folded hands for several minutes. Then at last she raised tearful eyes to look at Dr. Phillips.

"Are you quite certain?" she asked. She wiped her eyes with a tissue hastily offered by Dr. Phillips from a box on his desk.

Preston Phillips, MD, nodded sadly, his lips pressed together in a tight line. Moments passed. "I'm sorry," he said.

"How long do I have?" she whispered.

Dr. Phillips paused, then spoke slowly. "I'm not an oncologist, but I'm referring you to Milton Jones. He's the best guy in town for what you need." He paused. "It's not my field, Miss Thistle, but you need to get right on this. Please, please, don't waste any time."

He wiped the back of his hand across his eye. "I'm very sorry, Miss Thistle."

Miss Thistle closed her eyes for a few moments, then rose to her feet, certain the young doctor could sense her legs were trembling. She steadied herself by holding onto his desk. "Don't be sorry, Dr. Phillips," she said, smiling. She reached out to shake his hand. "I'm going to see Jesus. It makes no difference how I go."

Dr. Phillips returned the smile. "Don't give up so fast, Miss Thistle! There are things we can do." He picked up his telephone. "Let me call Dr. Jones to schedule a consult. He's the finest oncologist in the area and a good friend of mine. I know he'll schedule you for surgery right away."

Dr. Phillips began punching numbers, but Miss Thistle shook her head. "No," she said. "I need to seek the will of God first. There are so many things to consider, so many features to every problem. Surely you remember that from twelfth-grade economics class, do you not, Dr. Phillips?"

Dr. Phillips smiled. "I do indeed, Miss Thistle. As well as many other things you taught me. All right. I'll give you a week or so."

"We'll seek the timing of the Lord and His will in all things."

"Yes, ma'am," the doctor said as he walked her to the door. He slipped a brochure into her hand at the last moment. Miss Thistle noted the title, *Chemotherapy and You*, and sighed.

"At least read it, Miss Thistle," he said. "Sometimes complete remission is achieved. No more cancer."

"That reminds me of a Scripture verse," Miss Thistle replied, a smile appearing on her face. "'*Without the shedding of blood*,' the Book says, '*there is no remission of sin*.' Whatever this cancer does, I know my sins are in remission. That's certainly a blessing, isn't it?"

"Yes, ma'am," said Dr. Phillips as he opened the door and waved goodbye.

Miss Thistle's blue cotton dress *swish-swished* around her knees as she walked slowly to her car. She thought again about getting a cane to help her walk. No matter what she decided about treatment, there was no use compounding the trials of the upcoming months by falling and breaking a leg or a hip. What awful trouble that would cause someone, and she wanted nothing so much as not to be a trouble to anyone.

Settling herself into the maroon leather front seat was a relief. The sky was clear blue, the air fresh, the wind a soft breath on her skin.

"I'll be sorry to leave this beautiful old world," she said aloud. She laid her head down on the steering wheel for a few moments to gather some strength. When she placed her handbag onto the passenger seat, the purse tipped over, and the doctor's slick brochure slid halfway out.

At least read it, the doctor had said.

"Well, I'll do that much," she said. "And I'll find some time to pray this through!" She started her ignition and carefully backed out of the parking space.

Miss Thistle had seen more than a few people do battle with the enemy called cancer. It came in so many variations, so many levels of ferocity. Sometimes it hung around for years. Other times it pounced on someone and killed him in a few weeks.

She turned the car out onto the main street. Miss Thistle loved the fact that she drove a car. Her mother had never driven, leaving all the driving to Homer. It was entirely possible that Grandmother Alice had never ridden in a car. She had done nothing day and night but care for the sick and work with her hands throughout the harsh fifty-two years of her life. And Great-grandmother Ruth—who lived to be one hundred five, having begun her life as an American slave—had wanted nothing to do with cars or the twentieth century in general with its constant rushing hither and yon. Before Great-grandmother Ruth there was nothing but an endless, nameless line of women back through slavery, back across the sea.

A red light jolted her mind back to the present. Her gaze fell on the flashing time and temperature sign above the bank. It was twelve-fifteen already! Only forty-five minutes until the Superbrains assembly, and she had no team to announce. She sighed.

It must be God's will that we have no team this year, she thought. She thought about the doctor's chemo pamphlet. *Maybe God does want me to focus on my own health instead of the team.*

Chapter 3

Miss Thistle pulled into her reserved parking place, rushed into the cafeteria for a plate of food, and found a place in the teacher's lunch room, hoping to eat quickly enough to be able to gather her thoughts together before announcing there would be no team this year.

The Lord will see to it, she thought. Her mother had always told her to depend on the Lord Jesus in every single thing, large or small. *Cancer or school assemblies*, she thought to herself. *It makes no difference to Him. He's in control, and He is always good.*

She placed the cafeteria tray onto the table and pulled out a chair. The room was crowded and noisy as everyone talked about the day's events. Among other things, the Brocks' situation was discussed sadly.

"Thanks for saving me from my sixth-hour grammar class," Miss Tina Stevens said to her. "I lost myself in *Pride and Prejudice* last night and didn't prepare for class, so I'm glad for the assembly."

Miss Thistle smiled and toyed with her food. She wondered if she could ask the teachers to nominate their best students for the team or if she could simply stand before the student body and ask for volunteers for the Superbrain team. Neither of these obvious solutions seemed right.

She looked around at the teachers and staff as if she were committing them to memory. *I'm going to miss these friends*, she thought. *I'm going to miss this whole wide world.*

She smiled at Miss Stevens and said not to worry about it, that she herself had enjoyed Elizabeth Bennet's and Fitzwilliam Darcy's love story more times than she cared to admit even to herself.

Dr. Phillips's face suddenly rose before her mind, and she felt sorry for him. What a life it must be to give terrible news to people day after day; —people who, as she had been, were unprepared to hear it.

And why wasn't I prepared to hear it? she wondered as she picked at her green salad. *The whole world is chock-full of heart failure and stroke and cancer. Why should it surprise anyone at all to hear that he has one of these horrible agents of death lurking in his body? And, on the other hand, we are equally surprised when someone arrives disease-free at his one hundredth birthday! Everything surprises us: life, death, health, illness, joy, despair.*

The chair beside her was suddenly pulled out and Dr. Hamilton dropped heavily into it, tossing his brown-bag lunch on the table at the same time. "All ready for the assembly?" he asked.

"Oh yes, I'll be ready!" Miss Thistle said. She peeled her orange and ate it one section at a time. It was sweet and juicy.

Bethany Shore cleared her throat. "It's the Superbrains assembly again, is it?" She applied a new coat of bright-red lipstick with one hand while holding a mirror with the other. Then she rubbed her lips together and smacked them loudly. Principal Hamilton jumped at the sound.

Miss Thistle smiled. "It is."

"And this is your final attempt to get to the state finals, isn't it?" She clicked her mirror shut with a sharp snap.

Miss Thistle smiled at Bethany. "I suppose it is, yes." She had announced at the beginning of the school year that she would be retiring after graduation this June, completing forty-one years in service at Judson. Sometimes she wavered on that decision. After all, she was only sixty-one years old. Most people worked until they were older than that. But there were things she wanted to do, and who knew how long a person would have good enough health to do those things she wanted to do? Travel, short-term mission work perhaps? She had looked into a school in the Philippines and one on the island of Guam. And there would always be the possibility of returning to Judson on a part-time basis. Sterling had assured her of that.

Now, with today's diagnosis, all future what-ifs had dissolved into meaninglessness. Bethany's sharp questions interrupted her thoughts.

"How many applications for the team did you get? May I see them? Who is on the selection committee?" Bethany rattled off questions as if she'd written them down and memorized them.

Miss Thistle stared at Bethany for a few moments before answering. Such a pretty girl she was, with her perfect smile and thick wavy blonde hair. And yet, there was something harsh there, something Miss Thistle couldn't quite put her finger on. Bethany was certainly qualified to teach teenagers—in the sense that there were diplomas on her wall—but she lacked a gentleness that teenagers needed. It was ever so hard to be a teenager these days, wasn't it? They needed care and tending, rather like plants, whereas Bethany appeared to prefer what was called an in-your-face approach to life and teaching—almost combative, it sometimes seemed.

Miss Thistle knew that beginning teachers often needed to be bolstered by experience before they settled into the real work of educating even younger minds. It did seem though that although Miss Shore had grown a few years older, she hadn't really matured much. Too, she often felt that Bethany resented her own success, especially (it had to be admitted) how the students loved Miss Thistle. She wished she could convey to Bethany how such love and respect were gathered bit by bit over years, but Bethany did not often ask for advice, and certainly not from Miss Thistle.

"There weren't many applications for the team this year," Miss Thistle said, swirling water around in her paper cup before taking a sip.

"May I see them? Maybe a new sponsor would help us win. We never have won, you know." Bethany took another look at herself in her compact mirror, nodded approval, then stood and picked up her tray to return it to the cafeteria.

"Oh, but we did win," Miss Thistle said. She smiled at Bethany and folded her hands in her lap. "When I was a senior, we took first place. Class of 1967." Miss Thistle beamed as if the results had just been announced.

"Oh, yes, 1967!" Bethany laughed, as if the entirety of 1967 was inconsequential, even comic. She shrugged her long blonde hair over her shoulder and said, as if it were an afterthought, "Quite a few years between wins, wouldn't you say?" She paused before adding, "Plus, wasn't that before all the schools competed together?"

Bethany spoke so loudly that other conversations stopped and most of the faculty frankly listened in. The exception was William Ross, PhD, the bearded, bespectacled chairman of the history department. Dr. Ross's head was bent over a thick book. With one hand he traced line after line as he read, and with the other he held a peanut butter sandwich. He chewed slowly and read deliberately. Occasionally, he would lay his sandwich on the table, take up a pencil and write something in the book, as if correcting the text.

"For many years there were two Superbrains competitions, yes. In 1978, the contest was integrated," Dr. Hamilton said. "I was on that team. Miss Thistle was my coach. We took fourth in the state, I thank you very much."

Some applause erupted, and Dr. Hamilton bowed slightly, grinning.

"I'm just saying that if you want to win now—in the twenty-first century—maybe you should think about getting some fresh leadership for the team." Bethany said. "I'd be happy to help out. That's all I'm saying. For the honor of Judson Christian High School and all that."

"Miss Thistle will uphold our honor very well, I'm sure, Bethany," Dr. Hamilton said. "Now if you're interested in coming along beside her this year, watching how she works, and so forth, so you can head up the team next year after she's retired, well, that might be a possibility," said Dr. Hamilton.

"Play backup to Miss Thistle?" Bethany's eyes opened wide. "I have a master's degree in teaching. I've already logged three summers on doctoral coursework. Are you saying I need to learn from her how to teach five kids how to answer questions and how to smack a button quickly?"

"Bethany," said Dr. Hamilton. "That's unkind, and that's not what I said. I said Miss Thistle is in charge this year, as she has been every year."

"Sorry," Bethany said. "Oh, by the way, did you read today's *Ledger*? This year's Superbrain finals are going to be held at South University. If we do make it to the championship tournament, we're going to want a stellar team representing us. South U's president, Dr. Greenleaf, has agreed to preside."

"Dr. Thaddeus Greenleaf?" Miss Thistle asked in a whisper. She clenched her hands to still the trembling. A look of wistfulness passed over her face. Recovering quickly, she hoped no one had noticed the slip.

"Yes, Dr. Thaddeus Greenleaf, his very self," said Bethany. "So you see, you might want to consider having someone else—"

"That's enough, Bethany. Miss Thistle is in charge of the competition," said Dr. Hamilton.

"Fine, then. Forget I asked. I was only trying to help." Bethany Shore swirled out of the room, slamming the door behind her.

The other teachers resumed their individual conversations. Dr. Ross continued to read.

Sterling Hamilton smiled at Miss Thistle. "Sorry about that," he said. "How was your doctor's appointment? Any news?"

"It was fine," Miss Thistle answered in between bites of sandwich. "Nothing to worry about. And don't worry about Bethany. She's young. She'll mellow. I've got her on my prayer list."

They ate in silence for a while.

"Dr. Greenleaf is kind to do this for the high schools. It's a wonder he has time." He coughed. "I actually met him once."

"Really?" said Miss Thistle.

"Yes," said Dr. Hamilton. "He's quite the intellect. It was at an administrator's conference, and I said—" He paused, noticed Miss Thistle's distraction and asked, "Miss Thistle, are you all right?"

She shook herself back to the present. "I'm fine. Yes, perfectly fine. Everything's wonderful. Yes." She paused. "And Thaddeus will present the trophy!"

"Thaddeus?" said Dr. Hamilton. "You're on a first-name basis with the good doctor or something? Having lunch these days with presidents of universities?"

"Oh no," said Miss Thistle. "Nothing like that." She busied herself with eating.

"So," said Dr. Hamilton after he finished his lunch, "Who's on the team?"

"I don't know," said Miss Thistle quietly.

"You don't know? The assembly's in less than half an hour. Must be tough to choose among the applicants, hmm?"

Miss Thistle looked up into his face. "There were no applications," she said.

"None?" His mouth dropped open. "How are you going to make a team at today's assembly with no applicants?"

"I don't know. I've been thinking and praying for days, especially this morning. And, well, I still have a bit of time to think of a great idea. I'm trusting the Lord Jesus to provide me with the right leading. He always has before, and I'm certain He will today as well."

"Well, Miss Thistle, I trust the Lord too, but surely with only a few minutes to go before announcing a team, we need to put this thing into overdrive. I'll call an emergency meeting of the kids with the best grade point averages. We'll offer them something they can't refuse. We'll—"

"That's certainly a possibility, Dr. Hamilton, but if you'll just give me a little more time, I'm sure the Lord will provide."

Miss Thistle smiled and stood. She reached for her bag but missed the handles and knocked it over. The brochure from Dr. Phillips's office slid out onto the table in full view of Principal Hamilton.

Dr. Hamilton eyed it sternly. Then he looked at Miss Thistle, who deftly snatched the brochure and slid it back into her purse.

"What's that for?" he asked gently.

"That? Oh it's nothing. General information I picked up from Dr. Philips."

"You're not having chemo for anything, are you?" his voice was suddenly soft. Miss Thistle could tell that his mind had instantly whirred into action, thinking of hospital visits, pink carnations, tuna casseroles, coffins.

"Me? Chemotherapy?" Miss Thistle said. "What a thought!"

"Good," Dr. Hamilton said firmly. "I don't want my best teacher sick, that's for sure!"

Miss Thistle rose and left the room. She was smiling but felt so very tired, and she had not one glimmer of an idea on how to organize a team from a pool of nobody. Still, "He giveth more grace when the burdens grow greater!"

She heard footsteps trotting up from behind and was surprised to see William Ross fall into step beside her. Dr. Ross was well known never to speak to anyone without necessity although he was unfailingly polite when addressed.

"If I may," he said, "I would like to speak with you in your classroom for a few minutes regarding the Superbrain competition. I have a little theory."

"Why certainly, Dr. Ross."

Chapter 4

Four-hundred-fifty students noisily jostled their way into their assigned seats in the auditorium. Tim Barnaby slumped into his seat in row seventeen, and wished for the hundred-thousandth time that his parents would let him stay home and study through one of those online homeschool programs. It was easy. You did your work; you got your grades. No dealing with stuck-up kids, quirky teachers, or nonsensical assignments that didn't do anything other than waste good time. Tim stuffed his black backpack under his chair, then slouched as low as he could and crossed his arms across his chest.

It was a constant irritation to him that he was forced to sit between two girls. Jill Abbot and Emma Bryce were not only two of the most popular girls in school, they were also best friends who couldn't, or wouldn't, stop talking to each other. They talked around him, over him, in front of him, so that his exaggerated slouching, while being a defensive posture, enabled them to gossip with as little obstruction as possible.

Tim's opinion was that these two girls had the intelligence of sheep and the communication skills of parrots—*yackity, yackity, yack*—lots of talk, no meaning.

Tim sat up when Dr. Hamilton tapped on the microphone. "Stand, please."

Tim stood with the student body for the opening prayer, then sat down at the amen. It was amazing how much noise was created by half-a-thousand people sitting down. Chairs screeched on the tile floor; books fell; people talked. People could hardly stop talking, Tim had noticed, especially those of the female gender.

Dr. Hamilton introduced Miss Thistle, "the heartbeat of our school." Everyone had heard it before, but Dr. Hamilton rarely missed a chance to relate the events surrounding a firm paddling he himself had received from the hand of this very same Miss Thistle, "back in the dark ages" when spankings were allowed and when particularly intransigent children required a licking. "She had a stronger arm then," said Dr. Hamilton, "but not a stronger heart. Her heart beats for Judson Christian High. Let's give Miss Thistle a warm welcome."

Almost everyone stood and clapped, whether because they actually loved Miss Thistle and intended to honor her, or because standing and clapping makes a lot of noise and can take a long time, prolonging the assembly and thereby postponing the return to class.

Tim did not stand. He sat low in his seat. It wasn't that he did not love Miss Thistle. Who could not love her? He was simply so bored with school. It was as if there were a toggle switch in his mind that flipped down to *off* when he stepped onto the campus of Judson Christian High School. He didn't stand unless it was actually required. Besides, stomping and clapping irritated him. Girls liked to prate and squawk like birds; boys liked to stomp and shout.

The truth was, Miss Thistle was one of the few teachers Tim admired. Dr. Ross was another. Miss Thistle was the person who had introduced him to the *CIA World Factbook* back when he had her ninth-grade geography class. The United States Central Intelligence Agency had so much information on every country in the world that they let the easy stuff spill out onto their web site for anyone who wanted it. You could find out almost anything about anywhere. Tim gobbled up every bit of information he could from the factbook. He looked at that site almost every day when he got home from school and the energy switch in his brain tipped up to the *on* position. Who knew geography could be so interesting?

Back in middle school, he'd had a world history teacher who spent the first quarter of the school year on geography, mashing lists of terms—biomes, Arctic Ocean, ice caps, tundra, taiga, permafrost, isthmus, steppe—into their adolescent brains as if these were the things that mattered about the world! Tim grunted aloud, thinking about teachers who thought the difference between tundra and taiga was actually important. Something to be tested on!

The clapping and cheering over, Miss Thistle approached the microphone holding a sheet of paper. She cleared her throat and then tapped the microphone as if it had stopped working in the moments between Dr. Hamilton's introduction and now.

The clapping slowed to a stop, and Miss Thistle began.

"Each year the state holds an academic contest to determine which school has the best students. In 1967 Judson Christian High School won that contest! I was the captain of that team. This is my last year as team sponsor, and thus my last chance to repeat that brilliant result. Shall we win one for me this year?"

"Win one for the Thistle!" someone shouted. Miss Thistle nodded.

"Miss Thistle! Miss Thistle! Miss Thistle!" chanted the audience.

The boy behind Tim lisped, and the resulting "Mith Thithle!" so irritated Tim he turned the full one-hundred-eighty degrees around and glared the boy into silence. It was a small victory because Jill and Emma were swaying to the chant, causing Tim a wave of fear. If for some reason they were to sway in opposite directions, he would be crushed between them.

"Excellent, thank you," said Miss Thistle. She pulled out her sheet of paper. "On this paper I have the names of this year's team members. They have been chosen in a slightly different manner than I have previously employed. Normally, I am sure you know, I study the applications and make the decision on my own, but this year I had a little help from our resident school genius, Dr. William Ross. Let's give Dr. Ross a hearty Judson hand!"

Everyone clapped; a few students stood. Very few students actually understood Dr. Ross, but those who did swore his was the finest mind in all the county if not the state, perhaps in all of American history.

Dr. Ross stood and blushed. He knew himself not to be the finest intellect in the history of America, acquainted as he was with the works of Jonathan Edwards. He waved at the student body tentatively, offered a half grin, then pushed his black-framed glasses up the bridge of his nose and plopped quickly onto his front-row seat.

"Dr. Ross and I used a theory of his and some good old fashioned sense to determine this year's team. And, as you may have read in the morning *Ledger*, the great Thaddeus Greenleaf, president of South University will preside over the championship match, so we want only the best for Judson!"

After the clapping, a voice called out, "Tell us the team!"

Jill and Emma were holding out their hands in front of them so they could see and admire each other's fingernail polish. Tim cringed and tried to imagine the quiet peace of homeschooling.

He had once made a list of forty-five reasons he should study at home. Reason twenty-two was listed as "fingernail color conversations." Emma and Jill had once debated—over his head while he slouched—the perfect color of fingernails. Emma was certain that Blushing Rose was the best, while Jill had grown stubborn in her defense of Rich Scarlet! Tim shuddered remembering this and decided to move this infraction to number two or three if he ever reorganized that list.

Maybe if he had a different chapel/assembly seat he would not dread school so much ("Horrible seat assignment" was reason number six.) Surely there was a better way than the ABCs to arrange people. If men took women's surnames at marriage instead of the other way around, he would now be Tim Henson, which would have sat him between Chad Hancock and Brent Hessler, an almost infinitely better situation. Maybe he could make a special request. He would have to make up a health-related reason. The administration would never respect the truth that he simply could not stand these two girls. "Patience, Tim," they would say, or "Girls will be girls, Tim," or "Tim! These are beautiful girls!"

Beauty is fine, but he wasn't looking at them; he was hearing them. Still, Jill and Emma were not the only problem with having to attend school. The mass of hundreds of teenagers jostling, running, giggling, belching, and so forth disturbed his emotional balance. His mother had reminded him many times that he ought to be thankful for the opportunity to attend a Christian high school with so many Christian friends. Tim explained that even Christian kids—and a great many of them were not believers at all if you got down to brass tacks—giggled too loudly if they were girls and sweat and belched if they were boys. He did not consider the horrifying opposite truths that boys occasionally giggled and that girls have been known to sweat and even belch.

Tim loved his Saturdays when he could sleep until nine, eat a late breakfast with his mom and dad while his ten-month-old sister Dot played with her oatmeal and his yellow Lab Ike sat at his feet and waited for ends of bacon pieces. Mow the lawn, read a spy thriller, check out the CIA site, help Dad chop wood, build fires, catch a few footballs. A kid could learn a lot more in an environment like that. A kid could learn almost anything, but with gossiping girls distracting him—

"Our first team member is Andrea Weathers!"

There was a deep silence for five eternal seconds.

Miss Thistle tried again. "Come on up, Andrea. That's right, up here on the platform."

A trickle of applause followed Andrea as she mounted the steps and stood next to the podium. Her legs shook. Her eyes were wide with obvious fear.

"Leonard Luther!"

"What?" shouted Lenny Luther. "Huh?"

His fellow basketball players hurrahed and grunted as they pushed the six-foot-four athlete bodily up the stairs where he stood sheepishly next to Andrea. Andrea stepped away from him, her eyes now firmly fixed on the floor of the platform. Tim thought she might be crying, not that he blamed her. The idea of standing on stage in front of all these people and next to that thug Luther would make anyone cry.

"What is going on?"

Tim heard this question and looked up. Standing at the wall, perhaps four feet away from him was Miss Shore. Now here was a teacher he deeply disliked (reason number thirteen: "Miss Shore"). If he had time, he could make a comprehensive sublist—13a, 13b, 13c— of the things about her that bothered him. One of the most annoying was the way she chewed on her long hair when she thought no one was watching her. And the way she adjusted her framed diploma before starting class with her word-for-word class-starting prayer.

"What is going on?" Miss Shore repeated, this time clearly addressing Emma. "I just came in."

"You're late," said Tim, just under his breath. He slouched a centimeter or two lower in his chair.

"Miss Thistle's announcing the Superbrain team," Emma said.

"That basketball player is on the team?" Miss Shore sounded almost angry. "That one up there?"

"I guess," said Emma.

"Emma Bryce!" cried Miss Thistle from the platform.

Emma squeaked and jumped. She stumbled up to the stage where she stood next to Andrea, who was still crying.

"The final regular member of the Superbrain team is Arthur Fletcher!" Arthur was roundly cheered. Even Miss Shore clapped for him. He was well known as a math genius who possessed superb clarity of thought. He always sat in the front row in class and regularly startled teachers with incisive questions. *But Miss Stevens, don't you think Hemingway's worldview was more than a little rationalistic?* Arthur took the platform in a great leaping bound, straight over the front, not mounting the stairs. He raised both hands to the audience and bowed from the waist. "Thank you," he said loudly. "Glad to be of service." He punched Lenny Luther in the arm and grinned.

Tim surveyed the completed team from his slouched position. Not your ordinary Superbrain team, that's for sure. Except for Arthur, whose brainpower was undeniable, there wasn't one remarkable intellect up there. *Probably slim pickings*, he thought. *Maybe the smart people were too busy with college applications to apply. Or maybe they figured it's no use. We never win, anyway.*

Miss Thistle quieted the clapping students with a wave of her hand. "These four accomplished young people will comprise the regular team members," she said, "but of course there is a need for an alternate. In case someone gets sick, of course."

A short burst of random cheering was acknowledged by Miss Thistle, who then said, "Our alternate Superbrain is Tim Barnaby. Tim, come on up!"

Tim's heart froze as he heard his name being chanted by his classmates: "Barnaby! Barnaby!" He stood on shaky legs, plunged past Miss Shore and reeled up to the platform, Jill's voice following, "Are you OK, Tim?"

He acknowledged the crowd's wild acclamation—Tim! Tim!— with a tentative wave, then turned to Arthur and said, "But I didn't apply!"

"None of us did," said Arthur.

Chapter 5

"Great idea she had," Timothy Barnaby Sr. said, slapping his son on the back. He loosened his tie, slipped it over his head, and tossed it onto the kitchen counter. He took his place at the head of the table. "Miss Thistle was a wonderful teacher before my time, during my time, and even now," he said.

Tim asked his mother to please pass him the mashed potatoes. He took a big scoopful and flung it onto his plate.

"Well, I do think she might have warned us," Mrs. Barnaby said as she tried to insert tiny spoonfuls of mashed potatoes into Baby Dot's closed mouth. "Open," she said. "Aaahh." Mrs. Barnaby's mouth opened wide in an attempt to get Baby Dot to open hers but without measurable result. Dot grabbed the spoon and flung potatoes onto the floor where Ike quickly licked them up.

"Had I known Tim was going to be chosen for the team, I would have attended the assembly. I would have brought the camera."

Tim groaned. "Well, I'm glad you didn't come then. No offense, Mom," he said. "It was embarrassing enough without the camera and baby."

"Still," said his mother. "It would have been nice of her to let us know." She busied herself around the kitchen, sometimes sitting down to eat a little but mostly jumping up to check on things, get more food for the others, and coax the baby to open wide.

"I don't want to be a Superbrain," Tim said lamely.

"Yes you do. Everyone wants to be a Superbrain," said Mr. Barnaby. "It's like saying you don't want to be the star running back. Or you don't want to slam dunk the winning basket. Of course you do. Everyone does. I wanted to be a Superbrain, but I didn't have the grades. I was chasing your mother at the time, of course, which may have distracted me."

"Timothy!" said Mrs. Barnaby.

"The point is, everyone wants these sorts of honors," said Mr. Barnaby, grinning.

"I didn't," said his wife. "I never wanted to be a star football player." She swirled her corn kernels into her mashed potatoes then hopped up to look at the coffee. "But here's a true confession. There was a moment in my life I wanted to be an opera singer." Tim and his father both laughed suddenly, causing Baby Dot to startle and open her mouth. Mrs. Barnaby deftly slipped a spoonful of pureed peas into the tiny mouth.

"At least I'm being honest," Mrs. Barnaby said. "You should admit you wished you had ever returned a kickoff ninety-eight yards for a touchdown."

"Wouldn't that have been sweet?" her husband said softly.

"I would have cheered for you," Mrs. Barnaby said. "But then I cheered for you anyway."

After a few moments of silence, Tim said, "The point is, I don't want to do this. I don't want to be on the team."

His mother shook her head. "You are on the team, son," she said. "It's not like you're overly involved in other activities. I don't think you're involved in *any* other activities. This will be a good use of your time, and that's that." She spooned more potatoes into Dot's mouth.

"Mom's right, Tim," said his father. "You have to do it. You are part of the team. You, my son, are a Superbrain." Mr. Barnaby placed his hand over his heart. "Our beloved alma mater, Judson Christian High, has called upon you. You must answer that call."

He stopped to chew and swallow an enormous bite of meatloaf. "But I am wondering how you were selected. Do you know what criteria was used?"

"We're all asking that!" moaned Tim. "None of us applied. Plus, Miss Thistle said Dr. Ross helped her choose the team this year."

Mr. Barnaby threw his head back and laughed. When he caught his breath, he said, "Well, there you have it. William Ross, human computer. He was in some of my college classes. Of course, he was fourteen and we were all twenty! Blew us all out of the water with his perfect test scores!"

Tim choked and spat out green beans. "Fourteen!" he coughed.

"Oh yes, the man is as brilliant as a solar flare! Had his PhD at twenty-one, no lie. Thus, if he is one of the reasons you're on the team, then you're on the team for the best of all reasons."

"Talk about a superbrain," said Tim. "I'm sixteen. By the time he was my age he was graduating from college!"

Mr. Barnaby pulled a piece of paper and a pen from his pocket. "Who else is on the team?" he said.

Tim's mouth was full of food, but he managed to make the names understandable as he chewed. Mr. Barnaby listed them down the paper, one after the other. Then he asked, "Who is Andrea?"

"I don't know," said Tim. "She plays the piano for chapel sometimes. She's in choir. Fairly pretty, very shy. I've never even said hello to her."

"You'll be good friends now. She's the classical music and literature component. Who's next?"

"Lenny Luther."

"Son of Leonard and Svetlana Luther, right? Lenny Senior and I go way back. Okay, that's the European history and languages component. He's on the football team, so you automatically think he's not smart. Right? But look what goes on at home! Wide, rich culture, a plurality of languages."

It was decided that Arthur Fletcher had been chosen for his broad-based academic genius, in particular the maths and sciences.

"What about Emma Bryce?" asked Tim.

Mrs. Barnaby chuckled. "I know this answer," she said. "Her mother is the most social of all the town's social butterflies. Rumor is she met a Kennedy once! The fact is, Emma will know things about society and people in general that regular nerd-type brainiacs won't know in a million years."

"*Nerd-type brainiacs*?" asked Tim, staring at his mother.

"You know what I mean," she said, stopping to eat a few bites. "Smart people."

"The point is," said Mr. Barnaby, "she has a place on the team. All right. Good."

Tim sighed. "I really do not like that girl. She seems so, so . . ." Tim searched for the word, "so pointless."

"You should like girls by now, son," Mr. Barnaby said. "You're sixteen years old."

"I like girls fine, Dad," Tim said. "But the girls at school act so amazingly stupid. I hide when I see them coming. But then at assemblies and chapel, I'm stuck. Now I've got Emma and Andrea at Superbrain practice!"

"Okay, that's settled. Emma Bryce is our trivial social butterfly component. Which leaves you, Tim W. Barnaby Jr."

"Yeah, what about me?" said Tim. "Why am I the alternate? Out of ninety-seven juniors, why me? There are way smarter people."

"That is the most brilliant move of all," said Mr. Barnaby. "Next time I see Will Ross at the library I'm going to stand up and cheer. I'm going to pound him on the back. Think about it. You're the alternate. That means you have to fill in for any of the team members. Anyone gets sick, you're in."

"Yes?"

"Well, think about it. You know everything that can be known about geography and the countries of the world. You play a pretty fair piano. You have a smattering of math and science, and your brain is nimble and interested. Plus, you haven't been studying very much lately—I've noticed this—so it's like your brain's had a rest. It's ready to go! They couldn't have picked a better alternate! Makes me hope one of those other kids gets sick so you can have a spot at the table, pressing that button! I kid you not!"

Later on when Tim was in bed, Mrs. Barnaby asked her husband, "Why do you really think they chose Tim?"

"I have no idea," Mr. Barnaby said, "but my job is to encourage him beyond his own abilities. He'll be great."

Timothy Barnaby Sr. got a kiss for that.

Chapter 6

In a small brick house on Maple Street, Miss Thistle was having dinner with the Ross family.

"Do you think they'll revolt?" she asked. "It was pretty bold of us choosing names out a hat like that. If it comes down to brass tacks, we can't actually make them study the manuals."

William Ross didn't hesitate. "I've always wanted to test the theory that any ordinary kid can meet up to any reasonable expectation." He reached over to cut a young child's meat into small pieces. "Though I have to say I was more than a little relieved when Arthur's name came out!" He and Miss Thistle both laughed.

"They won't quit," he continued. "They'll stick with us. Kids will rise to what is expected of them. They'll be as great as any other team. Plus, all that clapping from their peers is good for the heart. People like to be applauded. They'll want to hear it again, and the way to do that is to stick with the team and work hard to win." William Ross grinned. "Human nature is the same everywhere at all times and places. People love to be admired and cheered. They'll take to this like ants to sugar."

"Like bees to nectar," said a boy.

"Like moths to a flame," said a girl.

Miss Thistle raised her eyebrows and looked at Dr. Ross.

William Ross blushed. "It's a little game we play here. Trying to get the kids to think widely and carefully. Similes are lovely things. Aren't they, Miss Thistle?"

"Yes indeed they are," she said. *What a nice family,* she thought. *I wish I could see these children grow up.* Now that this long day had reached its end, the events at the doctor's office grew gigantic in her mind. She struggled to keep her thoughts together.

William's wife Clara placed dessert in front of Miss Thistle's place. Vanilla ice cream drizzled with chocolate sauce, a couple of chocolate sandwich cookies on the side. "Yummy," said Miss Thistle. "Thank you for having me over tonight. I was feeling a bit out on a limb announcing those names like that."

"You are welcome here anytime, Miss Thistle," said Mrs. Ross. "We enjoy having you here. Don't we, children?"

"Yes, ma'am," said a chorus of young voices.

"Stay for worship?" Dr. Ross asked.

"With pleasure," Miss Thistle answered. There was something soothing, something eternal about worship at the Ross home. The cadenced answers to the catechism questions, the expressive reading of the Scriptures, the earnest prayers. Miss Thistle felt she was withholding herself when she prayed, as she did not mention her illness. *God knows,* she thought. *God help me die with grace.* She thought it might be unholy but whispered, "Please not until we win. Please let Thaddeus see us win."

When the children had been put to bed, Miss Thistle asked Dr. Ross if he thought Miss Shore had a point.

"A point?"

Miss Thistle nodded. "About the Superbrain preparation process needing fresh blood."

William Ross frowned. He cleared his throat. "Well, she may have had a point—I am not saying she does—but her delivery of her opinion was decidedly childish, regrettably so, I believe."

"Meaning she'll regret it or we will?"

"I expect both," said Dr. Ross. "She's leaning on her own understanding. Lean too far, you'll fall over."

"Mmm, true," said Miss Thistle.

"And her manner was combative. One wonders whether her reckless anger will take her places she should not go."

Miss Thistle nodded. "A city broken down, without walls."

"Exactly," said Dr. Ross. "Not a very defensible position."

Chapter 7

Miss Shore jabbed the air with the clear plastic fork. Two days had passed since the announcement of the Superbrain team, and she remained irritated.

"The point is, these kids did not apply! Their rights were violated! How humiliating to be shoved up on stage like that. If I were their parents—"

"That would be most awkward," said Miss Tina Stevens, the English teacher. "If you were their parents, that would make you plural, and my dear, although you may have filled out some since you came to us several years ago, I would hardly say you've reached plural dimensions."

Miss Shore blushed. "Very funny," she said. She laid down the brownie she was toying with and selected a carrot stick from the tray. "The point is, where does Miss Thistle get the authority to summarily appoint students to the team?"

"Settle down, Bethany," said Miss Stevens. "Miss Thistle's been doing this since before you were born. And although you probably know more than she does from a textbook perspective, she's really good with the kids. They love her a lot."

"That's true enough," admitted Miss Shore. "Still, I could get them to win."

There was a loud cough from the end of the table. All eyes looked to see Jose Garcia, the custodian, who said, "Um, ladies? Are you sure this is the place for this?"

"Hear, hear," said Coach Brock, back to school now after taking a few days off to comfort his wife. "Let's leave the armed combat to the football team, shall we?"

Miss Shore stood and placed her hands in front of her on the table. "Isn't that just like a man?" she said. "A couple of guys want to argue about something, that's okay; but two women start arguing, and it breaks one of the commandments or something!"

Mr. Garcia cleared his throat. "I'm just asking if this is the right place for it. Maybe we could have some prayer about it together, as a staff?" He sensed everyone's eyes on him and felt the weight of being "just the custodian" in a roomful of credentialed professionals. There was the sound of the door opening, but the conversation had so engrossed everyone, no one looked to see who had come in.

"He's right," said Miss Stevens. "We need unity as a staff. How can we serve the Lord if we cannot even have lunch together?"

Sandwiches were laid down on the table and a few heads bowed.

"I agree," Miss Shore said. "Let's pray that some good sense will prevail so we can get this competition done right for once."

"Bethany," a deep voice said.

Miss Shore whirled around to see her boss. "Dr. Hamilton," she said in a startled voice. "How nice of you to come. We were just going to pray for Miss Thistle to have wisdom in leading the Superbrains team since it seems she doesn't understand little things like getting consent before assigning kids to a semester-long project like her beloved team."

Dr. Hamilton said nothing but only looked at Miss Shore, who seemed to take his silence for encouragement to continue.

"It's like I was telling my senior economics students. Contracts require an offering party and an accepting party. Announcing a merger before one of the parties has signed off on the terms is grounds for annulment of the contract. In fact, several of my seniors said—"

"You spoke with your students about your concerns?" Dr. Hamilton's voice remained steady, but his eyebrows arched.

Miss Shore continued to speak, unmindful of her lack of discretion. "Well, you know a lot of the seniors are eighteen, and they need to understand these things. In fact, did you know one of the Superbrains himself—Lenny Luther—is almost nineteen, and I told him he has a right to—"

"Bethany," said Dr. Hamilton. "I understand your concerns. And it's true that you're very smart, and you'll be a great replacement for Miss Thistle next year if you'll sit with her a while and gain some pointers. But for now, let's give Miss Thistle time to work with this team before we pick on her process." He smiled. "She's been around a long time, and she may know a few things we don't about the psychological workings of the typical teenager's mind."

Miss Shore cleared her throat. "No, she doesn't know more than I know about that. My doctoral studies confirm that Little Miss Thistle is dead wrong here!" She leaned back against the wall and faced the principal as if she had decided to die defending this point.

Dr. Hamilton spoke softly. "The woman you refer to as Little Miss Thistle is one of my personal heroes."

"But she's not mine," Miss Shore exhaled loudly. "In my book she's an unqualified black lady taking us down the road to embarrassing public defeat for the forty-first time. Sorry. It's just my opinion."

"You'll have to excuse me," said Miss Stevens, gathering her things. "This conversation is too tense for me."

"Joining you in that," said Coach Brock. He and several others shoved back their chairs and left the room.

Miss Shore attempted to join the exodus but was stopped by Dr. Hamilton's hand on her arm. "Come see me in my office now," he said calmly. "I'll send someone to cover your next class."

Miss Shores eyes opened wide. "In your office? Am I in trouble?"

"Let's say we need to sit and have a friendly chat, all right? Five, ten minutes tops."

"Fine," said Miss Shore, whirling out the door, which slammed behind her. Dr. Hamilton looked around at the few members of his staff who were still lingering over lunches and quiet conversation.

"It wouldn't hurt to go ahead with that prayer meeting now, Jose," he said.

Ten minutes later, Miss Shore sat in the principal's office. She folded her arms across her chest and stared at the row of potted plants lining Principal Hamilton's top book shelf. She eyed his PhD diploma with envy.

Dr. Hamilton entered, greeted her politely, and laid a sheet of light blue paper on his desk. He studied her silently for a few moments, said, "All right, okay, fine," wrote for a second or two on the blue paper, folded the paper, and placed it in an envelope. He laid the pen down and folded his hands on top of his desk.

"Bethany," he said. "This isn't only about the Superbrains, is it? There's something else troubling you. Has someone said something to hurt you? Is there a problem you'd like to discuss, or something going on at home perhaps? "

Bethany pressed her lips together into a tight line. "No," she said. "I'm fine. Home's fine, though I wish I could move out of my parents' house. It's so hard not to be able to afford my own place even though I'm almost thirty."

Dr. Hamilton sighed and nodded his head. "That is hard, Bethany. Once your schooling is finished, you'll be done with tuition payments, and you'll get a nice raise for achieving your doctorate. That should help."

"Yeah," said Miss Shore. "I'll be able to move out for my thirty-first birthday. It's embarrassing to tell you the truth."

There was a short silence before Dr. Hamilton ventured, "Is there a spiritual problem you'd like to share with me, Bethany? I'm sensing you might not be fully engaged in our mission here. Not everyone is, you know. Judson isn't for everyone and sometimes it takes a few years to work that out."

"Are you saying you don't think I fit in here?" Miss Shore said.

"I'm saying you've been more combative about Miss Thistle and the Superbrains than I would consider normal." Dr. Hamilton tried to make eye contact, but Miss Shore looked away.

"So I don't fit in, and I'm not normal," she whispered.

"Bethany, you know that's not what I said," Dr. Hamilton said quietly. He put his hands together in front of his face and looked over his fingers at her. "Maybe you just need a few days off to clear your head." He chuckled. "That would do anyone good. I could use a break myself. Why don't you take the rest of the week off? Paid time, of course. Come back Monday and we'll talk, see what you've thought about."

Miss Shore stared at the ceiling for a few moments. She tapped her foot on the carpet under her chair. She reached for her purse. "I'm afraid if I take a few days off, I won't want to come back at all," she said.

"Why's that?" asked Dr. Hamilton. "Are you really that unhappy here? Is it Judson itself and not only Miss Thistle?"

"I feel strangled here," Miss Shore said, "I feel like no matter how I try, I'll never measure up. It's like my degrees and accomplishments mean nothing. And Miss Thistle! That little black woman without a bachelor's degree—she's the cat's meow around here."

"You might have noticed that I'm black as well."

"Yes, of course, but you have earned degrees. What does she have? One year at junior college!"

"And you wish you had the respect that Miss Thistle has earned over forty years?"

Miss Shore swallowed hard. "It's not easy teaching here, Dr. Hamilton. Maybe it would be better if I left." She looked around the office, still refusing to make eye contact with her boss.

"I didn't say that, Bethany. You need some time off. Doctoral studies are hard, and you have a full time job as well, plus the pressures of not being out on your own. It's no wonder you feel overwhelmed."

"I am not overwhelmed," Miss Shore said. "I am unwanted." She stood and grabbed her purse.

"Next Monday, we'll chat?" Dr. Hamilton said.

"No," said Miss Shore. "I'm clearing out my desk. I quit."

Dr. Hamilton dropped his head into his hands. "Bethany," he said. "Please." But the door had already slammed behind her.

When the door slammed, a rush of air blew a few papers off the desk onto the floor. Dr. Hamilton was so deep in thought he didn't notice. The secretary came in later and picked up the fallen envelope. She turned it over in her hand and smiled when she saw the address on the front. She sealed and stamped it and placed it in the outgoing mail.

The following week a quarter-page advertisement appeared in the *Ledger*. Miss Bethany Shore, BS, MEd, PhD candidate, and experienced teacher, would sponsor a group of independent students who wished to compete on an alternate team in the Superbrains competition.

Chapter 8

Miss Thistle sat behind her classroom desk knitting something pink and fluffy as she surveyed the four Superbrains who had arrived in her room and were now awaiting only the arrival of Arthur Fletcher for the meeting to begin.

Tim Barnaby jiggled one leg while he read the Superbrains rules manual. Emma Bryce stared at her pale pink fingernails, then toyed with her long brown hair. Andrea Weathers stared at the floor. Her fists were clenched in her lap. She appeared agitated, but Miss Thistle could not be sure. Young girls could be so emotional; it took almost nothing to set them off. Lenny ate crumb donuts out of a box, one after another.

Miss Thistle smiled but said nothing. Occasionally she would miss a stitch, say, "Whoops a daisy," gather the stitch back up and continue with the project. She hoped no one would ask her what she was working on as the answer would be completely awkward: *I'm knitting a lovely soft bed jacket in case I end up in the hospital with this cancer.* Nothing could be so ridiculous, and yet she hadn't fully discerned the Lord's will yet regarding treatment, and if she did become hospitalized, who could imagine going around in those gowns they provided?

Miss Thistle had known people who died of cancer after having every possible treatment, and she had known some who survived simply by changing their diet and adding nutritional supplements. It was a personal choice what measures to take, and she wanted to know what the Lord had in mind for her.

Thinking about her illness all the time was not going to be good for the team, she knew. Her father Homer would have told her to "set it aside, let it ride" until she knew for certain the Lord's will in the matter. She looked at his picture on the filing cabinet, then drew a piece of paper from the thin top drawer of her desk. She wrote quickly on the paper for a few moments, folded the paper in half, and slid it back into the drawer. She shut the drawer firmly.

Just then the door opened, and Arthur Fletcher burst in. A sigh of relief rose from the other four team members, as if he was the only hope for the team.

"Mr. Fletcher," said Miss Thistle, also with a great sigh. "You've come at last. Please be seated, and we'll get started." She smiled. "It's our first official meeting."

She prayed aloud for the team, for unity of spirit and growing friendships, for success.

After the prayer she coughed. "I suppose I shouldn't pray that we would win, but the Scripture does tell us to ask for the things we need. I surely would like to win this year. Dr. Greenleaf . . ." her voice trailed off momentarily, and then she caught herself.

"Ahem," she said. "Let's get started. I suppose we are all agreed that Arthur will be the leader of the team."

The Superbrains nodded, but Arthur coughed and said, "Alas, ma'am, as much as I'd be honored to serve in that capacity, I cannot. I propose Tim Barnaby, our alternate, as the leader."

Three seconds of silence followed this statement, and then a sudden choked sob was heard. Everyone looked to the sound. Andrea attempted to stifle her crying. "Sorry," she said.

"It's okay," said Tim. "I don't have to be the leader." He nodded over at Arthur, whose eyes were also wide and wondering. *Girls!* they thought.

"It's not that," choked Andrea, breathing hard. "I'm sorry."

"Don't you worry," said Miss Thistle. "We're a team in here. Take the time to gather yourself."

There they sat for a few minutes until Andrea was able to speak.

"I can't be on the team," she said. "I want to. Really. I wanted to apply for the team even, but I didn't because . . ." Her voice trailed off. She collected herself and continued. "I want to help the school" She looked at Miss Thistle. "And I want to help you win. But I can't!"

Andrea bent forward and rested her head on the desk. Emma smoothed down Andrea's hair and gave her some tissues.

"Let's confirm this has nothing to do with Tim being the team leader. Is that part okay?" Miss Thistle approached this softly.

Andrea nodded her head violently.

"Tim's fine," said Emma, interpreting the nodding.

"Good," said Arthur.

"Not good," said Tim.

Andrea whispered, "The problem is my mother." She swallowed hard. "If we go to tournaments and start winning, she'll come."

"That's excellent," said Miss Thistle. "We count on family support."

Andrea's voice could barely be heard as she said, "My mom is crazy." She looked up. "I mean it. She changes her hair color every week, and she wears crazy clothes. She'll wear bizarre hats and bring huge signs. I'll die of shame!"

Miss Thistle rose stiffly from her chair behind her desk and came around to Andrea. She put her arm around Andrea. She said nothing for a while, and the silence weighed heavily while everyone waited.

Andrea said, "She dressed as a clown once for a parent-teacher conference."

"Hmm," said Miss Thistle, quite certain clown apparel was inappropriate for a conference, at the same time wishing she herself had the nerve to try something new once in a while. Young girls embarrassed so easily, she thought. What might seem inconsequential to her could be of enormous concern to a girl Andrea's age.

At last she said, "Andrea. I'll leave this to you to decide. But I want you to know that what you see as crazy other people may see as fun. I wish I had the nerve to change my hair color or wear a fun hat!"

"Signs would be great," Emma offered. "My mother would never make a sign. I wish she would."

Andrea managed a feeble smile at Emma. "You don't know my mother's signs," she said, but Miss Thistle patted her shoulder.

"Hey," said Lenny, "Was it your mom who brought the 'Eviscerate the Vikings' sign to that game last year?" He guffawed. "Oh yeah, and remember that other one, 'Disembowel the Panthers!' That one had huge blood drops painted on it!"

Andrea nodded and blew her nose.

Miss Thistle glared at Lenny who said, "Sorry, but at least she comes to the games. Lots of parents don't even come."

Miss Thistle coughed and turned on Arthur, "Why is it," she said, "that you cannot, as you say, serve in the capacity as leader, so much so that you have already tossed that ball to Tim?"

Arthur grimaced. "Well, I'm a senior for one, and I have these tough classes, and then there's college applications. And . . . actually, my mom won't let me. She says I have enough to do. She said I could stay on the team if I was a member, but not as leader. She says things pile up, and there are responsibilities you don't know about, and people start asking you things, and . . ."

"Understood," said Miss Thistle. "Tim, then." She nodded and wrote on a sheet of paper.

Tim sat up straight. "So just like that I have to be team leader? I'm just the alternate. I'm not really on the team."

"That's even better," said Emma. "You could help all of us that way. You could take care of problems and help us study."

"Yeah," said Lenny, who until this moment had said little, busy as he was eating donuts and distressed as he was with the crying girl. Now he licked donut crumbs off his fingers. "Like the manager of the football team. He's not on the football team, but he makes sure everyone has what they need."

"Now I'm the water boy?" said Tim.

"No, stupid, the manager," said Lenny. "Can't you hear?"

"Mm-hmm," Miss Thistle cleared her throat. "None of that language. Are we agreed, Mr. Luther?"

Lenny wiped his hands on his pants and nodded. "Sure, Miss Thistle," he said. "Sorry."

"This is excellent," said Miss Thistle, tapping her pencil on her notepad. "Tim will operate as the leader in the sense of a servant-leader. The last shall be first, and so forth. Tim will lead the team to victory by assisting each one of you in your studies. He'll make sure you're studying. He'll urge you on. He'll telephone you and make sure you are on task and on target. Everyone write down your number and pass it to Tim."

Tim gathered the papers but asked, "Isn't it your job to urge everyone on to victory, Miss Thistle? Shouldn't I just be studying like the rest of the team? I mean, I have to fill in for anyone. I have to study everything."

"Yes," she sighed, "you're right. It's true that ordinarily I do the nagging." How tired she was. How completely unsuited to the task of whipping these five students into optimal mental shape! "But why don't I take a year off from badgering my team? I'm sixty-one, you know."

"You be the nagger, Tim," said Arthur. "Let Miss Thistle have a break."

Miss Thistle wondered again if Bethany Shore had been right. She wondered if Dr. Phillips was right. She wondered if —

"Miss Thistle!" said Arthur. "Earth to Miss Thistle!"

"Oh yes! Sorry, I distracted myself," she said. "Let's get down to business, shall we? We've agreed that all of us will stay on the team, is that correct?"

She looked around and everyone nodded. Andrea nodded firmly, wiping her eyes with the fistful of tissues.

"And Tim will be our staunch and fearless leader. Now, here are some study manuals for you, sample questions from other years, and so forth."

She distributed the books. As Mr. Barnaby had foreseen, math and science questions to Arthur; music and literature to Andrea; etiquette, history, and art to Emma; religion, languages, and athletics to Lenny. Then she gave Tim a copy of each of the books. When the bell rang signaling that first hour class would start in five minutes, Tim shoved all those books into his backpack. They barely squished in. Picking the pack up, Tim groaned under its weight and pretended to fall down. The boys laughed; Emma giggled. Miss Thistle noticed that Tim blushed when Andrea smiled at him.

Chapter 9

"After your county Superbrains tournament, Tim, we'll have the whole team to dinner to celebrate our victory," said Mr. Barnaby. He propped his socked feet up on the coffee table, shook the newspaper out in front of his face, and attempted to scan the news while talking.

"What if we don't win?" Tim asked.

"What do you mean 'if we don't win'? What sort of talk is that coming from the team leader of the Judson Christian High School Mighty Patriots Superbrains? Win? Of course, we'll win! Don't talk like that! And if we fail, we'll fail daring greatly, our faces marred by dust and sweat and all that. We'll exhaust ourselves in the trial, and thus need my famous barbecued steaks even more. Right? So it's settled. We'll win, and I'll barbecue!"

Tim nodded. "That will be great, Dad. Thanks."

"Janet, buy some steaks." He looked back at the newspaper. "Look here, did the Cyclamen win? Does anyone know?"

The paper rustled and jumped as Mr. Barnaby attempted to find out how his favorite team had done in last night's game. He grunted as if disgusted and laid the paper aside. "Well, never mind that. Let's talk about the barbecue. Do Superbrains eat steak? Are the girls vegetarians?"

"All girls are vegetarians," said Mrs. Barnaby. "At least they all go through a phase of trying to be one. I know I did when I was a girl. Someone paints a lurid picture of cows mooing contentedly, being led in an unsuspecting line to their inevitable, violent deaths. Bingo, a girl loses her appetite for meat. *The poor cows*, she thinks."

"Gross, Mom," said Tim. "Contentedly mooing cows going to their deaths."

"My point exactly," his mother replied.

"But you're not a vegetarian."

"I got over it. I realized I liked hamburgers more than I was sorry for the cows."

The paper rustled, and Mr. Barnaby rejoined the conversation. "Oh, too bad, the Cyclamen lost," he said. "Why can't they win?"

"They're five years old, Dad. It's T-ball. How many grown men follow T-ball teams?"

"You've got to follow someone, and once you decide you're not going to slobber after those guys who make millions of dollars and pump illegal pharmaceuticals into their bodies, your choices are limited. It's a choice. I choose to cheer for the Cyclamen. They lost to the Geraniums. How could they lose to the Geraniums?"

"How could they have names like Cyclamen and Geraniums?" asked Tim. "Who came up with names like that for baseball teams?"

Mr. Barnaby laughed. "The same people who don't like contentedly mooing cows being led to their inevitable deaths. They change the Braves and the Warriors to the Geraniums and the Cyclamen. At least the name Cyclamen could remind you of a cyclone so there's some of the violence left."

"Mothers," said Mrs. Barnaby. "It's mothers who do this, if you want to know. We have an interest in raising children who are not immersed in violence."

"Back to the barbecue," said Mr. Barnaby. "Tim, you need to sound out the Superbrains and ask them if they eat meat. I don't want to buy seven or eight steaks if we're only going to eat three."

"Lenny will eat three by himself," said Tim.

Mrs. Barnaby stacked blocks on the floor with Dot. Dot squealed when she knocked the stack over, and the stacking began again.

"So call them up, Tim. I'm a small businessman—no, check that, I'm the owner of a small business—nothing small about me, is there?" Here he grinned and patted his ample stomach. "I'm not entirely made of money here, and I want to get the right number of pieces of meat. Do I need eight, ten, or three? How many of us are there?"

"There are five team members, plus you and Mom and Dot—who is too little for steak—and Miss Thistle, and of course Dr. Ross. He's a big help. He comes to practice when Miss Thistle can't make it."

"And his family!" said Mr. Barnaby. "They'll all come. It's a Saturday, and he won't leave his family alone on the weekends, so they'll be here. He's got a whole quiver full, as they say, plus his wife of course."

"There is no way she eats meat," said Tim. "She's very soft and sweet."

"I eat meat," said Mrs. Barnaby.

"And you are very soft and sweet as well," said her husband.

"Thank you," said Mrs. Barnaby. Her eyes narrowed at him. "How soft?"

"Perfectly soft," her husband said, smiling at her.

"So I'll call," said Tim. His father nodded, but Tim didn't move to the phone.

Tim's fear of the telephone, especially in relation to calling girls, could not be measured. For a moment he was relieved of the chore, however, when his mother asked, "Why is Miss Thistle not attending all the practices? She has always been the glue that held the Superbrains together."

"I think I'm the glue this year," said Tim. "She said why doesn't she take a year off? I don't know. She seems slower and sort of forgetful. Her mind wanders. Arthur's always saying, 'Earth to Miss Thistle,' like she's not really with us."

"She's been teaching for forty years, give her a break," said Mrs. Barnaby, carefully placing an alphabet block on top of a stack of five other blocks. "I hope when I'm her age I'll be allowed to slow down a bit."

"You can be slow now, dear, if you'd like," said Mr. Barnaby. "We promise not to say a word about it."

He winked at Tim, who grinned and started walking around the room in a slow, ponderous march. Dot abandoned the blocks and followed her big brother on her hands and knees.

They all laughed. Mr. Barnaby said he'd love his wife more than the earth itself no matter how slow she was. He folded her into his arms. Tim was embarrassed at this tenderness, so he scooped Dot up and stacked blocks with her until she knocked them over and squealed. Then Mr. Barnaby called Tim back to the present.

"Call the team," Mr. Barnaby said to Tim. "We've got to figure out the shopping list."

"Now?" Tim said. His throat swelled practically shut at the very thought of calling Andrea. The others would be easier, but Andrea!

"Now!" shouted his father. "Let's go! The meet is Saturday, so our victory barbecue is Saturday afternoon, which is only three days away, plus we've got to buy everything."

"Can't I just ask them at school tomorrow?"

"No, because you'll forget, and then we'll run out of time. There's not unlimited time here. We've got to plan."

Tim called Arthur first. "Are you a vegetarian, Arthur?" he said. "My dad wants to know." He explained about the Saturday victory barbecue.

Tim hung up the phone. "Arthur eats meat."

"Of course, he does," said Mrs. Barnaby. "All men are carnivores."

Lenny Luther's phone went unanswered. "Never mind that," said Mr. Barnaby. "I myself once had a hot-dog stuffing contest with his father. It was during the eighties. A lot of crazy things happened in the eighties."

The call to Emma's was short. Emma was not home, but her mother was able to say that yes, it was okay for her to go to the Superbrain barbecue on Saturday and yes, as far as she knew Emma would eat almost anything you put before her. "Frankly, she's a pig, but don't tell her I told you."

"Her mother says she's a pig," said Tim.

"Girls need to eat too," said Mr. Barnaby. "They try not to let you know it, but why do you think they have overnight parties? So they can eat in peace with no boys watching."

"We're not supposed to know they eat?"

"You're not supposed to know *how much* they eat. You're expected to think that a human body that weighs one hundred and twenty-five pounds is sustained on lettuce and water."

"Oh brother," said Tim, rolling his eyes. He instantly wondered if Andrea weighed a hundred twenty-five. He himself weighed only a hundred twenty. How ashamed he would be to find he weighed less than her! He walked to the kitchen and grabbed a few leftover rolls from the fridge. He frosted them with jelly and began munching furiously.

A few minutes passed in which Tim did nothing but eat standing in front of the open refrigerator while Ike pressed against his leg hoping for crumbs or handouts. The only sound that came from the living room was Dot's babbling and the banging of her blocks together. Tim sloshed down the bread with a huge glass of milk and wondered if the football players were right that if you mixed raw eggs—yuck—into your drink that you would become a hugely muscled he-man, surely weighing far more than a hundred and twenty-five pound female you thought you might be falling in love with.

He pondered the dilemma of drinking a disgusting, possibly salmonella-poisoned milk shake with only the faintest possibility that it might put some weight on his scrawny frame in what would probably be a foolish attempt to get Andrea to notice him.

He jumped when his father touched him on the shoulder. "Are you going to call Andrea, or do I have to?"

Tim's heart pounded so hard he could hear it. He looked at his father blankly. "Huh?"

"Ah," said his father. He rubbed his chin. "I see. I instantly divine your predicament."

Tim nodded. "I can't," he whispered.

"Then I will," shouted Mr. Barnaby. He lunged for the telephone.

"No!" shrieked Tim strangely, as if strangling. Then, "I'll do it," he said in a flat, going-to-the-guillotine resignation. His fingers shook so hard while punching the numbers that he misdialed twice. At last he managed.

"Hello, this is Tim," he said.

Pause.

"Can you come to a victory barbecue at my house Saturday after the tournament?"

He mouthed to his father, *She's asking her dad.*

"Oh, good. And, uh, are you a vegetarian? Because my dad is buying steaks, and he needs to know how many to get. No, it's not a problem, he just needs a count."

Pause.

"Okay. Thanks. Bye."

Tim hung up the phone, then collapsed onto the ground. "I'm dead," he said in a hoarse whisper. "I've called Andrea Weathers."

Mr. Barnaby stood up and retrieved a piece of chalk from the junk drawer in the kitchen. He drew around Tim's inert, stupidly-grinning form on the linoleum. "Yes, officer, I'm afraid it's a clear case of death by pretty girl."

Chapter 10

Three days later the Barnaby's large backyard was full of whooping, cheering teenagers and grinning grownups.

"You shot them out of the water!" shouted Mr. Barnaby as he plunked steak after steak onto the grill. "You launched them into outer space!"

He thumped Dr. William Ross soundly on the back. "Whatever selection criteria you used, Ross, it was a winner! Best team ever chosen at Judson Christian High, I kid you not!"

"*Were* winners," said Dr. Ross. "Criteria were winners; criterion was a winner. Criteria is plural."

"Of course, it is. I knew that," said Mr. Barnaby, turning back to his steaks and shouting more and heartier congratulations to anyone who passed by the barbecue.

"You gave it to them!" he said. "You blasted them to the stars! No one's better than you!" He tied on a white apron with the words *Kiss the Cook* imprinted across the chest.

Mrs. Barnaby smiled and congratulated everyone from her post behind a table laden with potato salad, tossed salad, Jello salad, corn on the cob, green beans, and rolls.

"Thank you, Janet, for putting all this together," said Miss Thistle. "It's a real treat. I don't remember ever having such enthusiastic parent support. At least not in the last twenty years."

Miss Thistle sat in the covered swing next to Dot. She pushed off with her toes to put the swing into a gentle back-and-forth motion while Dot showed her one toddler toy after the other.

Dr. and Mrs. Ross pulled up lawn chairs next to the slowly swaying swing. "The kids did great," Dr. Ross said. "Nice quick touch on the buzzer. You can be proud of them."

"I'm proud of you!" said Miss Thistle. "And grateful. Without your skill in choosing the team and all those extra hours . . ." She turned to Mrs. Ross. "Thank you, Clara. I know William isn't home enough as it is—what husband is?—and I thank you for allowing us to have a few more hours of him each week."

"You're quite welcome," she said. She smiled. "You remember he's a teacher; we get him all summer!"

There was a short silence, then suddenly Lenny shouted, "Hoo-boy! Did you see that team of Miss Shore's? Ha! I don't think they practiced once! What a bunch of complete losers." He scoffed loudly and stuffed a cornbread muffin whole into his mouth, crumbs everywhere.

"Lenny!" said Miss Thistle, "Let's be charitable. They did their best."

There was a long pause while Lenny chewed and swallowed and wiped his face. "Sorry," he said. "But after what Miss Shore said to you that day in the teachers' lounge, I haven't been her biggest cheerleader."

Dr. Ross wiped his mouth with his napkin, then placed it beside his plate and asked carefully, "Lenny, how, pray tell, is a senior student privy to the conversations in the teachers' lounge? Hmm, Lenny?"

"Uh. Oops," said Lenny, and there was a deep silence during which everyone stared at him. He ate another cornbread muffin slowly.

At last he said, "Let's say a scared little bird told me. Freshman kid my brother knows—new kid this year—was wandering down the wrong hall at the wrong time. Is that enough information?" He grimaced and stared at his plate of food.

"That's enough," said Dr. Ross. He sighed. "What people never realize is that walls don't have ears, but students do, and they can pick up a lot of things through very old walls. The whole student body probably knows how ungodly the staff was behaving that day!"

"Nah," said Lenny. "Nobody knows. The kid was so scared of what he'd heard, he only told my brother, who told me, and that was the end of it. Don't worry. Poor kid's so afraid he'll get suspended for eavesdropping on the teachers having a fight, he's still shaking!"

"The point is," said Miss Thistle gently, "do you think Miss Shore will be all right?"

"I don't care if she is all right," said Emma. "First of all, I never liked her. Who does? Plus she quit her job and left us with substitutes who come and go, so we are basically slumping through senior government and test prep. I already have to take the SAT over—my fault, I wasn't prepared—but now I get subs who don't know how to help. So I don't care if she's all right, sorry."

"Why'd you flunk the SAT?" asked Arthur. "What was your score? When are you taking it again?"

"You can't flunk the SAT, dummy," said Lenny. "You know that, Mr. Valedictorian. You just get a score, okay? Everyone knows that."

Arthur cleared his throat. "For you information, I do know that. And for your further information, I am not the valedictorian. I bow to Miss Jaycie McPhail and suffer in silence as the salutatorian. Second place, alas."

"Hey, why aren't you the valedictorian?" said Tim. "You are by far the smartest person in the whole school."

"Yes," said Miss Thistle, "Why is that, Mr. Fletcher? Is it our fault? Is Superbrains studying taking away from your grades?"

"No, Miss Thistle," Arthur said. "It's not that."

"Well, what is it then?" she asked. "Why is Miss McPhail the valedictorian and you are not? Did you get a B+ in advanced placement astrophysics?"

She hated that a brilliant student like Arthur could be denied the valedictory position because the classes he took were so rigorous almost no one could pass them. Some schools had gone to a different system whereby those classes received more grade points, but Judson Christian High School was not among them. Miss Thistle thought this hampered the future of deserving scholars, but she didn't say so.

"I got a B in cooking!" Arthur said, eyes shining. "My mother said since I refused to learn cooking from her I was required to take it at school. But I can't keep my mind on my boiling vegetables. Again, alas."

"It's a pity," said Miss Thistle.

"Indeed it is," said Arthur, nodding.

"What's a pity is that the meat's done, and you're all yapping over there. Come and get it!"

Mr. Barnaby was ignored for the moment as everyone discussed Miss Shore's failed Superbrains team at length.

"They didn't know anything!" said Arthur. "It was truly sad."

"It was truly great," said Lenny. "And I'm truly glad she's truly gone from the competition."

"Truly said," said Tim, proud of himself for this addition to the conversation.

"Her team really knew almost nothing. And they were slow getting to the button when they might have known. You have to buzz in quick!" said Lenny.

"We need to distribute these steaks quick!" said Mr. Barnaby.

"Quickly," said Dr. Ross.

"Quickly then," said Mr. Barnaby. "Let's eat. Ross, will you thank the Lord for this day's victory and the food?"

"With pleasure," said Dr. Ross. He beckoned his children, gathered them close around him, and then said, "Let us give thanks."

"Our Father in Heaven," he prayed, "we give thanks for so great salvation granted to redeemed sinners by the blood of the great God and Savior, the Lord Jesus Christ. Forgive us our sins. Receive our gratitude for our win this afternoon and for this food which Your hand has given us. Make us humble. Make us good. In Jesus' name we pray. Amen."

The Ross children repeated, "Amen."

Plates were piled high, Mr. Barnaby bringing a full plate to Miss Thistle so she would not have to get up from the swing. "My dear lady," he said, handing her the full plate.

"My goodness!" said Miss Thistle. "How's a body supposed to eat such a feast?"

"One bite at a time," said Mr. Barnaby happily.

Miss Shore's team and their devastating loss continued to be thoroughly discussed over the dinner.

Miss Thistle wiped her mouth with a paper napkin. "You'd think after all these years I'd have more people skills than I do have, but the honest truth is I'm as glad as everyone else is that she's done with the Superbrain competition. I admit she makes me nervous."

"There's no need for you to be nervous, Miss Thistle," Dr. Ross said. "She's the one who should feel awkward."

"Well, either way, at least she won't be at the tournaments still to come," said Miss Thistle. "Now that her team has been eliminated, there will be no reason for her to attend the meets." She paused, then added, "The poor girl has so much to learn that simply cannot be learned by trying to prove herself to the world."

After a while, Mr. Barnaby shouted, "Hello out there! There's a lonely steak here on my barbecue! Who didn't get one?" There was no answer, so he began to wander around looking at each plate. "Lenny Luther," he said at last. "You've got nothing but piles of salad on your plate! What gives?"

"I'm a vegetarian," said Lenny, blushing.

"What?" said Mr. Barnaby. "Is this something your mother brought from the Ukraine? Is this something you've got from studying the Bible? The pre-Flood diet? What?"

"No," said Lenny. He shook his head sadly. "It's how they kill the cows," said Lenny. "I read about it. It's really awful." He shuddered. "They lead them down these chutes, as if it's one more happy day on the cow farm, and then bang, they're dead."

"Well, I never!" said Mr. Barnaby. He wrapped the last steak up for the Rosses to take home.

They sat outside as the day cooled and talked about their victory until it began to grow dark. Every question was remembered and reviewed, who had said what.

"I thought I'd mess up on those prophets. I'm always confusing Elijah and Elisha," said Lenny, trying to balance green Jello salad on his fork.

Arthur cleared his throat. "I didn't think I would miss anything."

"And you didn't," said Dr. Ross. "You guys were great!"

"As I foresaw," said Mr. Barnaby. "Hence the victory barbecue, planned in advance. Well, Miss Thistle. What do you think of this year's Superbrain team?"

"They are wonderful," she said. "Like icing on my cake."

Dr. Ross prodded a child who said, "Like lemonade on a hot day."

"Like flowers in winter."

"Like sugar in tea."

The sky grew dark. Emma's father arrived to collect her. Then Lenny's parents came and stayed around to talk for a while. Arthur had his own car, and he left when the Luthers left. Only Andrea was left, so she helped Mrs. Barnaby clear up and put the dishes away.

"I'd better call home," Andrea said at last, wiping her hands on a checked kitchen towel. "Maybe Mom forgot me. She gets busy and forgets things sometimes."

Mrs. Barnaby handed her the phone, and Andrea pressed the numbers. After a minute she said, "Hi, Dad, it's me. Did you forget me? I'm at Tim Barnaby's house for the barbecue." She listened. Tim walked in and leaned against the wall. He gave her a questioning look. "Okay," Andrea said quietly. Then, "Okay" again. Then, "Bye." She hung up, then said to the wall, "We won, Dad."

"What is it?" said Mrs. Barnaby. "Are you all right, honey?" Tears came to Andrea's eyes, and Mrs. Barnaby wrapped her up in a hug for a long minute.

"Mom was collecting bugs again," said Andrea, hiding her face in her hands. "She makes lampshades with bugs glued on. People buy them on the Internet. Go figure. Anyway, she forgot about the tournament and the barbecue and me. They asked if you could take me home. Mom's up to her elbows in glue and beetles."

"Of course, we'll take you home, honey," said Mrs. Barnaby. She smoothed Andrea's long hair. "And they didn't forget about you. You are everything to them. Don't ever forget that. Parents love their children so much it hurts. Don't you ever think they forgot you. Come on, Tim. Let's take Andrea home."

Tim sat in the back seat and listened to his mother pour kind words and loving words on Andrea's wounded heart all the way home.

"Trust in the Lord, Andrea. In my experience, He's always been faithful. He'll be faithful to you too. Put your trust in Jesus alone. Cast your care on Him."

By the time Andrea got out of the car she was smiling softly.

"Thank you. For the ride and the comfort," Andrea said.

"Remember you're a victorious Superbrain tonight!" Mrs. Barnaby called after her.

"Bye," said Tim, but Andrea had already walked away.

After a silent ride home, Tim said, "Mom, you were great talking to Andrea."

"Thanks, Tim. I was just thinking how I would want someone to care for you if I couldn't. That's all."

Tim hugged his mother tightly, realizing he hadn't done such a thing in a few years. "I love you, Mom."

Chapter 11

Tim stared at his tennis shoes. He stared at the clock. He rolled pencils across the top of the desk in his homeroom class. At three minutes until eight, his hands began to sweat in anticipation of the upcoming school-wide announcement. At two minutes before the morning bell, he sat on his hands to keep them from shaking, and at one minute til, he cleared his throat the very smallest amount possible to make sure his voice wouldn't break when he gave a little speech of thanks after the back pounding commenced. He had actually practiced a short thank-you speech while skateboarding to school that morning.

The static crackled. Any second now, Dr. Hamilton's voice would come over the intercom to announce that the Judson Christian High Superbrain team had emerged victorious from the contest of the preceding Saturday. The basketball team's occasional wins were always called "emerging victorious" or "reigning supreme" over whichever "hapless foe" they had "trampled underfoot" a couple of nights earlier. It was widely reported that after these adjective-laden announcements, the athletes in their various homerooms were heartily jumped on and pounded with congratulatory slaps and loud cries of praise.

So it was no wonder that Tim sat on his hands and cleared his throat. He steeled himself to be jumped on by enthusiastic classmates. A girl might even hug him, he thought, before realizing this was a ridiculous and foolish hope. Still, anything might happen. The Superbrains' win at the county meet was far more prestigious than a simple ball-in-a-hole game.

"Quiet for the announcements," Miss Stevens said just in time for Dr. Hamilton to say, "Welcome to Monday morning, Judson Christian High!"

Tim's class replied, "Hi, Dr. Hamilton," as if the principal could hear them.

"Congratulations are in order—" Tim could hardly breathe now— "to Coach Brock and Mrs. Brock on the adoption of a baby girl this weekend. Let's give the Brocks a round of applause."

Miss Stevens blinked several times, blew her nose, and said, "Well, well. What a wonderful surprise!" and the class cooperated with loud applause and shouting, "It's a girl!" and "Will she play football?" Tim could hear cheers and clapping from nearby classrooms as well. His own clapping released some of his own nervous energy, and he was smiling broadly now in anticipation of the next announcement which was the one he had been waiting for. He was about to emerge victorious.

"More congrats are in order," said Dr. Hamilton. "Our very own Judson Christian High School Superbrain team took first place in the county tournament, beating out fourteen other teams." Tim felt his face turn a blistering red as Dr. Hamilton read the names of the team members. He stared at his desk and awaited the onslaught.

It did not come.

The boy behind him poked him with a pencil and said, "Good job, Barnaby," and that was all. Tim looked up, embarrassed. No one looked at him or even paid much attention to the announcements. It was business as usual at Judson Christian High! Even Miss Stevens, although she nodded at him in acknowledgement of this grand achievement, did not make a big deal of it.

"I thought I was going to cry," said Emma as the team gathered to eat their lunches together that day in the crowded cafeteria. "Remember how we were cheered at our first assembly when we were all shocked we were on the team? And now that we're excited to be on the team, no one else cares."

"I did cry," said Andrea. "But I cry so often, no one connected it with the announcement at all. One girl gave me a tissue and said, 'Sorry, is your mom okay?' No congratulations. Only a sorry!"

Arthur's story was similar. Only Lenny had gotten pounded and back slapped.

"I'm in the locker room for homeroom, so it doesn't count," Lenny said. "They'll jump on a guy in there for anything."

Sandwiches were chewed in silence around the table.

"Miss Thistle cares about us," said Emma, toying with her salad, stabbing a cherry tomato with her fork. "And Dr. Ross. He cares."

There was more silent chewing of sandwiches and sipping of juice.

At last Arthur said, "Well, Tim, you're our staunch and fearless leader. What do you have to say? Where's the heavy encouragement?"

Tim swallowed the last bite of his sandwich and took a great gulp of milk from the tiny house-shaped box. He slammed the milk box down on the table. "What I say is, we were great whether anyone else cares or not, and if we perform at that same level again at the regionals, we're going to get ourselves to the championships. I kid you not!"

"You sounded just like your dad when you said that," said Lenny. He folded a sandwich in half and stuffed the whole thing in his mouth.

"I was trying to," said Tim. "That's what my father would say. I was trying to be fearless. But truthfully, I feel rotten. I thought there would be balloons and a special assembly to congratulate us. I wanted to emerge victorious or reign triumphant."

Arthur agreed. "We didn't even save the day or uphold the honor of Judson Christian High School. We only 'won.' Dull!"

Everyone laughed halfheartedly and continued to chew. The ordinary noise of hundreds of people talking filled the cafeteria, but it was silent at the Superbrains' table.

"Hello, Superbrains." It was Dr. Ross. He pulled out a chair and sat down. "I thought I'd find you all here together bemoaning your unlauded state."

"How did you know?" asked Arthur.

Dr. Ross laughed. He removed his black-framed glasses and wiped the lenses diligently with his tie. "Me? How did I know that stellar academic achievement is not applauded with the same raving lunacy that follows a contest in which Team A puts a ball over a goal line or into a hoop a few more times than Team B? How did I know that intellectual prowess is not slobbered over in the same raucously indecent manner that occurs when—for example—a few boys line up, run as fast as they can and one of them is faster than the others? How did I—"

"Okay, all right, Dr. Ross," laughed Arthur. "We get it. You've been there."

Dr. Ross chuckled. "You have no idea," he said. "I am the poster boy for the unheralded brainiac. I know all about it."

Tim nudged Lenny in the ribs and said, "He graduated from college at sixteen!"

"And got not one parade for my trouble," grinned Dr. Ross.

"He got his PhD at twenty-one," Tim said.

"Did you get a parade for that?" Lenny asked. "That's pretty amazing!"

Dr. Ross leaned back in his metal folding chair. "No, no. No parades for that either. Of course, this was back before it was generally acknowledged that high school nerds do eventually—may I say it?—emerge victorious and run the engineering, scientific research, medical, and computer-related industries of America. My parents even caught flak for letting me finish college so quickly."

"Who said bad things about your parents? What did they say? Who do I beat up for this?" said Lenny.

"*Whom*, Lenny," said Dr. Ross. "It's *whom* do I beat up, but there is no need to beat people up. My parents understood. They continue to understand, now that I teach." He laughed again. "Those same people—the ones you'd like to assault, Lenny—now say, 'Why doesn't Will use that fantastic brain of his?' They think I'm not using it since I'm just a teacher."

"That does it," said Lenny. "I am going to hurt someone."

Dr. Ross leaned further back in his chair in a casual way that would certainly have resulted in a scolding or at least an archly raised eyebrow had a student attempted the same maneuver in his classroom. "My parents took it in good grace. They knew my heart was in ancient Mesopotamia and Egypt, not at football practice or high school dances. They let me follow my heart. They never felt pressured to make me do normal kid stuff."

"Did they make lampshades out of bugs?" Andrea suddenly asked. "My mother follows her own heart in that way." She stirred her juice with a straw.

"No, but my father still plays a fairly mean kazoo at all family gatherings." He smiled at Andrea who groaned, "Don't tell my mom. She would so do that!"

Arthur Fletcher cleared his throat. "Uh, Dr. Ross?"

"Yes?"

"Congratulations on getting that PhD. You must have worked really hard. You totally deserved a three-mile parade."

Dr. Ross removed his glasses and wiped the back of his hand across his right eye. "Thank you, Arthur," he said. "That's very kind of you." He cleared his throat, stood, and made a loud clattering putting the chair back under the table.

"So keep up the good work," Dr. Ross said. "You guys did great. Quite a few of us are very proud of you."

"Thanks, Dr. Ross."

It was much the same in the teachers' lunch room. The photocopying machine purred, clunked, and banged as it copied, collated, and stapled. Quarters dropped noisily into the vending machines. Quiet conversations took place around the table. When Miss Thistle entered, there were a few offhand congratulations tossed her way.

"Nice work, Miss Thistle," said Miss Stevens.

"Good job, Miss Thistle," said Mr. Garcia. "We are all proud of the kids. On to regionals next, is that right?"

"Thank you. Yes, regionals are next," Miss Thistle said. "But what I really want to know is how the Brocks are with their new little one."

"They are ecstatic," said Mr. Garcia. "Maria and I dropped by Sunday afternoon after church. We are expecting a little one of our own in a couple of months, and she wanted to hold that baby girl the moment she heard the news. I've seen a lot of women with new babies, but I've never seen a happier woman than Heather Brock. She's elated. Coach is off on family leave for a month!"

"God bless them," said Miss Thistle. She chewed on a celery stick and hoped the fiber and whatever else was in it would do something good for her. She'd done a lot of Googling over the past couple of weeks. Turned out a lot of people had much to say about curing cancer, even in its later stages. Celery was a main ingredient in one diet. She chewed her celery stalk thoughtfully. She didn't like celery—for starters, it was so stringy—but it sure was easier to stomach than the whole idea of nasty chemicals dripping into her arm day after day.

Then, wondering at how quickly one could switch from thinking about new babies to thinking about chemotherapy, she worked hard to focus on the joy that Heather Brock was experiencing at this precise moment. "Her heart is filled up at last," Miss Thistle said aloud. "Such a great joy a new baby is."

"Yes," said Miss Stevens. " 'Hope deferred maketh the heart sick, but desire accomplished is a tree of life.' "

Many teachers said amen to that, and Miss Thistle wondered if her own hope deferred was unworthy of her, indeed if it were worthy of the Lord's notice. Did she want to win the Superbrains contest for herself or for the students? To make up for having not seen Thaddeus for thirty-nine years? To make him proud of her?

She was still wondering when she went home that afternoon.

Chapter 12

Later that night in her tiny brick house a mile from school, Miss Thistle pulled her plush pink terry-cloth robe tightly around her.

She eased herself into the ancient La-Z-Boy recliner she had rescued from her father's possessions in the days following his funeral, when the men of Hope Zion Church of Jesus the Redeemer had brought their trucks to haul everything away to give to the poor. This had been required by their pastor's—her father's—will.

"The very poorest people will benefit," Homer Thistle's will stated. "No one else would want it anyway. But Magnolia Jane gets the house and the pictures."

It was true that no one but a truly needy person would consent to own the furniture that had been Pastor Homer Thistle's. It was so old and dilapidated, and yet, when the men were getting their arms around that recliner, Miss Thistle stepped in. "No, not that," she said. "I'll be keeping that."

She'd always kept it in a special place in the living room, and now she sat in it each evening when she had her final cup of tea and her fiber cookie to finish the day. She adjusted her weight in the chair to get more comfortable. "I've been sitting in this chair ten years, and Daddy sat in it for forty years before that. Who ever heard of a fifty-year-old recliner?" She'd had it recovered from the faded, worn dark blue to a soft patterned pink.

"Whoever heard of a pink recliner?" she said aloud. She pulled at the hand lever to extend the footrest. "That's better," she said, now much more comfortable. Her legs ached less when elevated.

She took her china tea cup from the delicate crocheted doily on the end table beside her. As she sipped the hot drink, the day's tension drained from her. She closed her eyes for a few moments to ponder her day.

She thought about the Superbrains, how hard they were trying to win their competitions. Arthur Fletcher with his brilliant steel-trap mind; Lenny Luther killing himself over those Latin and Greek word roots, prefixes, and suffixes; the girls with the music and the European kings; and Tim Barnaby with everything. The kids were working so hard, she thought. Maybe too hard. She'd seen their faces, knew it wasn't easy juggling school and Superbrains.

Her mind shifted to her cancer and the information she had read online about people her age undergoing chemotherapy. She wished her father and mother were there to help her through this decision as they had helped her through so many others before.

Miss Thistle looked around the dark paneled walls of her den. Family photos that dated back to the late eighteen hundreds covered the walls. She wished they had smiled in portraits in those days. It would have brought the people to life, made you understand who they were so much more than you could with those stiff poses with unsmiling expressions. There were also many newer photos, with smiling people. Miss Thistle herself smiled out from several.

"Stop reminiscing," Miss Thistle commanded herself. She chastised herself for not improving the time with godly meditation and gulped down the rest of her tea. She commanded herself to think happy thoughts about everything.

Even about the cancer. Going to heaven ought to be a happy thought, but try as she might, Miss Thistle couldn't find anything happy in that tiny tumor that was intent on killing her. Dr. Phillips had been certain that things didn't look at all good. She didn't have months and months to think about this, he'd said when he gave her pamphlets on "treatment modalities" and referred her to Dr. Jones, the golden boy of local oncologists.

Miss Thistle had driven by Dr. Jones's office twice. The first time she went to make sure she knew where it was, and the second time was to get "some leading from the Lord" on whether she should make the appointment, but Miss Thistle had driven on and then chided herself for asking for signs.

She got another cup of tea to fuel her evening meditations. How she loved her cozy house with its dark wood, its worn carpet, all of it gracefully aging around her, with her. The thought of cancer and treatments and great oncologists faded. She gazed around the room at the familiar photos, allowing her gaze to come to rest on a small framed photograph on a bookshelf. She knew her mother would have chided her for leaving that particular photo in her living room for so many years. She herself knew it was verging on inappropriate to have it there, but something inside wouldn't let it go, the picture of the handsome young man and the smiling girl.

Inside, one feels eternally nineteen, she often thought. *Nineteen had been such a lovely age. So young. So beautiful. So hopeful. So able. So in love.*

The doorbell rang.

"My goodness! What a moment!" She dropped the footrest on the recliner, and hastily pulled her pink robe around her.

The doorbell rang again. "Coming," Miss Thistle called. She looked through the peep hole, said "My goodness!" and opened the door.

"Come in, Andrea! My goodness, dear, what is the matter?"

Chapter 13

Mrs. Barnaby knew something was wrong with Miss Thistle. "I can sense it, Timothy," she said into the telephone. "A woman can tell this sort of thing. I think she's sick, but she's not telling because she doesn't want anyone to worry."

Mrs. Barnaby bustled around the kitchen while continuing to talk to her husband on the phone. "Believe me," she said. "I know what I'm talking about. I don't know how I know, but I know." There was a pause, then Mrs. Barnaby said, "No, no, enjoy yourself. I'll be fine here. Take your time."

She hung the phone up, and then pulled a casserole dish out of the oven just as Tim walked in carrying Dot. "Sorry she's dirty, Mom," Tim said. "I wasn't watching where I was going, and Dot slipped in the mud. I can put her in the bath."

Tim held out his little sister to show his mom the muddy little legs.

"No, I'll give Dot her bath," Mrs. Barnaby said. "It's fun for me to see her splashing around. You take the car and run this casserole over to Miss Thistle, will you, please?"

Mrs. Barnaby grabbed the car keys from the counter and tossed them to Tim before carefully gathering Dot. She nodded at the casserole. "Put it in a Tupperware before you go."

"You're letting me drive—alone? At night?" Tim stammered.

"Sure, why not?" Mrs. Barnaby said, with a studied thoughtlessness, as if flicking a piece of fuzz off her shoulder, "you can do it. Nothing to it. It's only two miles away, all easy streets. There's a piece of cherry pie too all set to go in the fridge. Take it along."

"Yeah. Great. Thanks, Mom!"

Tim knew the way to Miss Thistle's house. He passed it every time they went to the grocery store. It was a tiny square brick house surrounded by a perfect green lawn and a white picket fence that could use a fresh coat of paint.

The rumor was that Miss Thistle herself had built that fence back in the nineteen eighties when some concerned church members had urged her to get a dog because of gang activity in the neighborhood. She said she didn't need any dog. She said the Lord Jesus would watch over her, but she accepted the animal when it was given to her.

The gang members left her alone after she shouted at one of them, "Cory, shame on you. You have left the will of God to consort with these bad boys." Still she kept the dog and even grew fond of it. When pranksters dumped some rotten vegetables in her yard one Halloween, Bluto got sick and died.

After that, so the story went, she decided not to put a poor animal through something like that again, and she had been without a dog ever since. Tim's father had told him this, mimicking Miss Thistle's voice, *If I can't trust Jesus to take care of me, I surely cannot trust a dog stupid enough to eat rotten vegetables and die of them!*

Tim thoroughly enjoyed the quiet drive to her house. He felt independent and powerful, alone behind the wheel. He was, however, deeply relieved when he saw there were no other cars parked in front of Miss Thistle's house, which saved him the backing-and-forthing of parallel parking. He wished there was someone there to witness his solo driving achievement, but it couldn't be helped. He opened the passenger door, got the food out, and bounded up the steps where he knocked loudly.

When Andrea opened the door, Tim dropped the food.

"Yikes, oh sorry!" Tim dropped to his knees to pick everything up. Everything seemed to be intact (except his pride) though probably smashed (like his pride).

"Never mind!" said Miss Thistle, fumbling for the plastic tubs. "Casserole cannot be smashed. It is smashed by definition. And pie is none the worse for a little dropping. Don't worry about it at all. Nothing spilled; no harm done."

She tut-tutted around, her superbly attuned social antennae quivering with understanding. She wondered if even Dr. William Ross could calculate the odds of two obviously twitterpated students arriving unbidden at her house at the same time. And her in a terry-cloth robe!

Such an awkward scene! How was one to extricate oneself from such a to-do? She had to change into clothes, but she could not in any sort of conscience whatever leave the two of them alone in her living room while she did so.

"What shall I do?" she whispered, under her breath. The robe was entirely inappropriate for company!

Suddenly there was a very loud banging on the front door. Without thinking, but merely acting, Miss Thistle said. "Tim, get that and deal with it. Please! I have to get some presentable clothes on!"

She stumbled down the hall as quickly as her fatigue and sore joints could take her, feeling the ludicrousness of the situation keenly. Miss Thistle wondered who was at the door, completely trusted Tim to send them away, and changed as quickly as possible, trusting that the people at the door would hold Tim's attention for enough time for her to change so he and Andrea would not be left alone.

She laid the old robe over the back of a chair and pulled on a simple cotton dress. She heard rising voices and hoped Tim was okay.

When she bustled down the hall, the noise increased, stopping abruptly when she entered the living room.

Miss Thistle found herself in her living room staring at Mr. Barnaby and the entire Superbrains team.

Chapter 14

"My goodness!" said Miss Thistle looking around. There hadn't been so many people stuffed into her living room in years.

"Hello, Miss Thistle!" said Mr. Barnaby cheerfully. "We brought you some ice cream to go with that pie Tim drove over! I had to see how well he parked! Couldn't leave well enough alone, that's me!"

"My goodness," said Miss Thistle. Hospitality trumped all other emotions, and she quickly hurried to the kitchen to pull out plates and cups. "Come, come, everyone. Let's eat that ice cream! Let me just throw together some hot chocolate."

The story emerged that Andrea had arrived because her mother was "gassing cockroaches with Raid" while her father, who hated bugs in general and cockroaches more than anything, had hurried to the garage pretending the spark plugs on his old MG suddenly needed changing.

"I couldn't be there," Andrea said, "and I didn't know where else to go. I don't have any friends left since I started spending so much time on the Superbrains."

Andrea had thought about Emma on the walk over, and though they hadn't been friends before Superbrains, Andrea did have her phone number and called her with her cell phone. That explained Emma's being there. Emma sat close to Andrea nodding through the story.

"And of course, I came right away," said Emma. "Speaking of no friends, that would be me also." She laughed nervously. "You know how Dr. Ross's always saying, 'Get the facts down!' Well, I'm missing parties to get the facts down." She looked at Andrea and smiled. "But I would've come anyway, even if I had been at a party."

Andrea nodded her thanks.

"But what about the rest of you? And Mr. Barnaby? My goodness!"

"Well, that's a different story. The boys and I were at the Cyclamen game over in Eastside—"

"You were with Arthur and Lenny at the Cyclamen game?" Tim asked. "What in the world?"

"Long story!" Mr. Barnaby said.

It turned out Mrs. Barnaby had needed the car that morning and had dropped her husband off at work. One of his employee's children was a Cyclamen team member, so the two men had driven together to the game.

"And we went because your dad had talked about the Cyclamen so much at the barbecue, and we got to thinking," said Lenny.

"We got to thinking that he might be right about how you can choose whom to root for, and you can get just as excited about a T-ball game as you can about a professional game. And it's true!" said Arthur. "Who would've thought it? Then we saw your dad at the game, and we said we'd drive him home. We figured we could bum some dessert off your mom." Arthur grinned.

"And when we got there, we heard you were here. Your dad thought you'd need a ride home after the excitement of driving at night."

Tim rolled his eyes. "Yeah, right," he said, although the smallest, tiniest part of him was grateful.

"And did they win?" Miss Thistle asked suddenly.

"Who?" everyone asked.

"The Cyclamen."

Mr. Barnaby pounded the table. "They absolutely won. It was fantastic." The boys echoed his cheer.

Miss Thistle stared around at the unexpected gathering. "Well then," she said. "Let's have ice cream."

As they ate, Miss Thistle listened. She began to hear among the conversations a certain theme. No more friends. No time to study for school. Got a B on my last test. Missed three parties. Not sure about the college of my choice.

It was all said in good humor, but Miss Thistle knew that was because they were in her home. They wouldn't have even alluded to these disappointments had they been able to stop themselves: "Out of the abundance of the heart, the mouth speaketh." Miss Thistle knew they would not be speaking this way if there was anything else on their minds to say.

She stirred her ice cream until it was creamy and then took small bites and listened. What the kids were saying was true. They were studying day and night for a competition they had not signed up for. She herself had shanghaied them in public, practically daring them not to participate, then subjected them to morning and afternoon practices which they had faithfully attended. They had met her expectations, and even surpassed them with that great victory last weekend, but it had stolen their social lives and threatened to ruin their GPAs.

Suddenly her heart burned. "I've been so selfish," she whispered. All of her pushing the kids to study, her desire to keep Miss Shore off the team so she could orchestrate it alone, her desire not to get medical treatment so she could be alert for the meets. It had all been about her need—no, her *desire*, her selfish desire—to impress someone she once knew who probably didn't even remember her. So foolish. But there was a way to fix it.

She said brightly, "Let's quit."

"Huh?" Arthur said.

"You're right. You have all been overworking yourselves studying for a team you did not apply for, to win a contest you had no interest in. I say you've done your best. You succeeded. I'm proud of you. Now, back to your lives, your parties, your regular school studies."

"You're mocking us!" said Tim.

"No, I'm not," said Miss Thistle. She scooted her chair back from the table and surveyed them. She nodded firmly. "You've done well. You've done enough."

Emma lifted her head. "You mean it?" Everyone knew that Emma, as the most social of them all, had missed the most activities.

Miss Thistle smiled. "Yes, I mean it. Bless your hearts."

"This is the most ridiculous thing I ever heard!" shouted Mr. Barnaby. "Did I hear Miss Thistle, the heartbeat of Judson Christian High, use the word *quit*? Have you lost your mind?" He stared at Miss Thistle as if at an alien.

"No, I haven't." She took another small taste of ice cream. "Perhaps I have found it. These kids have gone beyond the call of duty. They're missing out on their lives. I say they should enjoy their lives."

There was a faraway look in her eyes, as if she had let something precious go and then found that it didn't hurt as much as she'd thought it would.

"So that's it. We quit," Miss Thistle said firmly.

"But we won the county meet," Mr. Barnaby said.

"Yes, but it's a small county," said Miss Thistle. "Anyone could have done it. Miss Shore could have done it if we hadn't been there."

"If her team had been prepared," said Lenny, scraping the remains of the ice cream out of the carton with his spoon.

"But the school is counting on us," said Emma halfheartedly.

"The school doesn't care that much," Miss Thistle said, snapping her fingers.

"But you want to win again before you retire," said Andrea.

"Oh, never mind that," Miss Thistle chuckled. She waved her hand as if to dismiss the thought. "A few years from now I'll be so forgetful I won't even remember the win of sixty-seven. Or maybe I'll think I won every year. So it doesn't matter at all."

She stood. "So it's agreed," she said. "The Judson Christian High Superbrain team is hereby disbanded." She smiled and took another taste of her ice cream. "Yummy," she said.

"This is the most ridiculous conversation I have ever been a part of," said Mr. Barnaby, and he shook his head at Miss Thistle and bundled Tim out the door and into the car.

Emma and Andrea watched as the boys drove away.

"Let's have a cup of tea, just us girls, before you leave, shall we?" said Miss Thistle. As she bustled about in the kitchen,

Andrea joined her, leaving Emma to look at pictures on the wall until they returned with steaming china tea cups.

"Miss Thistle, can I ask you a personal question?"

"Sure, honey."

"It's not my business, but is this you in this photo? It looks like you."

Miss Thistle joined her looking at the framed photo on the bookshelf. "It's nice of you to recognize me in that young face," she said.

"Who is the man? Is that your brother?" asked Andrea, looking over Emma's shoulder at the photograph.

Miss Thistle smiled and took a sip of tea. "Let's just say that man was a very special friend."

The girls looked at each other.

"Ooh," Emma said.

Andrea said, "As in a boyfriend?"

"Never mind the specifics," said Miss Thistle. "Let's have our tea."

The girls sat on the couch, but they grinned and giggled so much, Miss Thistle finally gave in. "Oh all right," she said. "There was a boy. We were young—nineteen to be exact—and we planned to get married. It didn't happen. We went on with our separate lives. But it's a lovely picture, don't you think? So I keep it up. Call it an old lady's silly nostalgia."

"That's it?" Emma asked. "That's the whole story?"

"No," said Miss Thistle, "but that's all I'm telling. Now you girls get home before your parents start worrying."

She hustled the girls out the door, shut it quietly behind them, then sat heavily in the pink La-Z-Boy, and turned her thoughts to prayer. *The team is disbanded. It's time for me to deal with my illness. Dear Father in Heaven, I need to know Your will. Shall I aggressively treat this cancer? Or is this tumor Thy divinely-appointed messenger to bring me home to Glory?*

She prayed for an hour but remained uncertain.

"Well, then, it is the will of God that I not know His will at this moment," she said. "I can trust Him whether He gives me a clear answer or not. But I am going to have to make a decision very soon."

Chapter 15

"So, that's it. We're finished. We are no longer Superbrains," Tim announced the next morning. The team had met out of habit for morning practice even though they were no longer practicing.

"It's good I can study again and not lose any more points on my GPA," said Andrea.

"Back to throwing parties," Emma said. She twirled her long hair and stared at the floor.

"Back to throwing the discus," said Lenny, confronting his daily boxful of donuts as if they were enemies to be defeated. "Metal Frisbee is what it is."

"Back to not filling out college applications," said Arthur.

"What's that supposed to mean?" Tim said. "I thought you were going to Yale or Harvard or some fancy school like that."

"Nah, not next year," said Arthur. "I'm taking a year off. Gotta make a little money."

"That's ridiculous," said Andrea. "You'd get a full scholarship. You are only the smartest person in this whole town."

"True enough," said Arthur, "but I'm taking a year off anyway. It's my grandmother's fault actually. She says most people spend their whole lives wishing they were one step ahead of where they are. Elementary kids wish they were in junior high. Junior highers wish they were in high school. High schoolers wish they were in college. Single people wish they were married, and so on. Grandma says she absolutely insists that I take a year off. She calls it a *gap year*, so I can work and think about what I want to study."

"That's crazy!" said Andrea.

"That's what everyone says," said Arthur, "but what I notice is that everyone in my whole class is stressing about college apps and SAT scores, and I'm not. I'm living my senior year to its fullest. I say to myself, 'Self, what is the hurry? Those ivied halls and big brick walls are not going anywhere.' Plus it was good not to have to worry about all that college stuff when we were studying for the Superbrain contest."

"Except now we quit," said Lenny, talking with his mouth full, dropping crumbs, as usual.

"Well, it's good we quit," said Arthur. "Still, it was extremely cool to be a Superbrain even for a while. We should probably write her a thank-you letter for all her help, leave it on her desk, and get back to our lives."

"Agreed," said Lenny. He smacked his lips and wiped his crumby hands on his pants.

"I have pink paper," said Emma.

Strangely, no one had a pen. There were number two pencils in abundance, but everyone agreed that a note to Miss Thistle should be written in pen.

"I guess I'll have to snoop," said Tim, "being your fearless leader and all." He got up and walked to Miss Thistle's desk. There was no pen on top of the desk, so Tim opened the drawer. "Now I feel like I'm stealing," he said, but the others said, "You're only looking for a pen. Miss Thistle won't mind."

Tim opened the drawer. A folded sheet of paper blocked his sight of the drawer, so he removed it, saw a few pens, and took one. As he moved to replace the paper, it fell from his hand and opened. One look told him he shouldn't read it.

But he did.

"Toss the pen here. Hello, Tim, the pen!" Emma urged from the back of the room.

"Hold on a second," he said, scanning the paper.

He cleared his throat. If there was a time to be a fearless leader, he reasoned, this was it. "Lenny," he said in a strange, authoritative voice. "Check the hallways. Is she coming?"

"Of course not, you moron. She doesn't come until eight."

"Just check."

Lenny checked while the other ex-Superbrains converged upon the front of the room. "What is it, Tim?" said Andrea. "What's wrong?"

"This is what's wrong," he said, shaking the paper in front of them. "Look, it's a secret note she wrote to herself. Listen."

"If it's secret, we shouldn't know."

"Sit down and listen," Tim said.

"It says, 'I have cancer and need treatment, but these students need me first. To everything there is a season. Superbrains first."

Tim folded the paper, placed it back in the desk.

"She's dying," said Andrea. "And me crying on her doorstep as if I've got problems!"

"Don't say that," said Emma.

"It's strange," said Tim. "She's the person who really wanted to win the Superbrains, not us. We didn't even apply. There must be some reason she wants to win."

"Whatever it is, it must be important," said Arthur. He looked around at the group. "Maybe we should think about that."

"What are you saying?" Emma asked.

Arthur sighed. "I'm saying, winning this thing means a lot to Miss Thistle, but last night when she said we could quit, she was thinking of us first."

Tim looked around at his team members. "Maybe we should put her first," he said.

"Yes," said Lenny. "Let's win her a championship."

Thirty minutes later Miss Thistle was surprised upon entering her classroom to hear the steady hum of question and answer, question and answer.

"May I ask what is happening here, my good friends?"

"We're studying, don't interrupt us," said Arthur, waving her off.

"For?"

"For the Superbrains competition," said Tim, "if you must know. We won the county meet and regionals are next weekend, remember? We don't have forever to prepare."

"But I've just met with Sterling—with Principal Hamilton. He fully understood when I explained that you'd had enough."

Tim interrupted her. "Unexplain it, please, Miss Thistle. And would you please keep it down?" He grinned at her. "We're studying over here."

Miss Thistle shrugged her shoulders in wonder. What could have occurred to work such a turn of heart in five teenagers? She sat heavily in her swivel chair and opened her drawer to get a pen to cross the date off her desk calendar. The drawer was open the smallest amount, which she thought odd, but then she'd been in a bit of a hurry to get away yesterday afternoon—doctor's visit and all—so she'd probably left it slightly pulled out. She crossed the date off her calendar, pulled her phone out of her purse and called Dr. Hamilton.

"Sorry to bother you like this," she said, "but I don't have the energy to walk back to the office. Forget everything I said this morning about the team. Everything's back on." Her heart was happy. Her face shone.

The kids met for lunch that day as usual, and for once they were glad about the isolation they had found so abhorrent yesterday. They jabbered over their food with such excitement that a few people stopped by to ask what was up.

"Hello? We're the Superbrain team. Did you miss that?" Tim said to one questioner. "You might have heard we won the county meet, and next weekend we'll win regionals. Try that on for size!"

The boy walked away shaking his head. "Talk about fearlessly leading, Barnaby," said Lenny. "But you could've been nicer to him. It's not his fault he didn't know what we were talking about."

"Nicer to him? Did Lenny Luther just say I should be nicer?" Tim asked. "What a day this is."

"I'm only saying," said Lenny. "Kid's a friend of my little brother."

"Nice to see you so animated," said Dr. Ross, sitting down heavily, openly scowling at them. "I heard you all up and quit.

Dr. Hamilton told me early this morning. So break it to me carefully and gently. My five best hopes for Judson Christian High to emerge victorious and reign triumphant pack it in after one truly horrible day, and now here they are apparently rejoicing in their liberty. What is up with this?"

He glared around at them as if they were utter failures, far below a level where such as he should notice them. He was, he admitted later, truly angry.

"But, Dr. Ross," said Arthur, "we won the county meet. Isn't that good enough for you?"

"Of course not. It's like a football team quitting before the playoffs, like walking out halfway through your SAT's, like—"

"Like leaving before dessert," said Lenny grinning.

"Exactly," said Dr. Ross. "And what are you all smiling at me about? This is no smiling matter."

"It will be when we win regionals next Saturday."

William Ross sighed deeply. "Really?" he said. "You're in?"

"We're in," they said, five faces beaming.

No one in the cafeteria that day could remember having heard William Ross shout before, and certainly nothing so absurd as, "Woo hoo! Superbrains rule!"

Chapter 16

Andrea Weathers snuck into the auditorium and walked up onto the stage. It was not completely dark because light shone through the side windows, but it was sufficiently dim to aggravate her fear.

She had been fearful ever since Miss Thistle had mentioned that the regional meet was a much bigger event than the county meet. *You can expect several hundred people at the final round. And I know you'll be in the final round!*

Several hundred people! The only time Andrea had been up in front of any great number of people had been that day a few months back when she'd been unexpectedly called onto this very stage. She remembered how her legs had trembled under her to the extent that she thought she might fall off the stage.

Emma had tried to calm her. "You'll be sitting down at a table," she said. "And it's not like you'll be making a speech. You just sit there and press the button when you know the answer."

Still, Andrea got permission to practice speaking on stage during the quiet afternoon when everyone had gone home. It might help. It might not. But at least it was worth a try.

She climbed up the steps and walked out to the middle of the stage. She looked out across the darkened room with its six hundred chairs and began in the loudest voice she could muster: "Four score and seven years ago our fathers brought forth upon this continent a new nation, conceived in liberty and dedicated to the proposition that all men are created equal. Now we are engaged in a great civil war—"

A door slammed and the lights suddenly blazed on. "Hey, who's up there?" shouted a girl's voice. "What's going on in here?"

Andrea looked down to see a girl she knew to be the captain of the varsity cheerleading squad. She was wearing her cheerleader's purple and gold practice outfit. The ever-timid Andrea lost her ability to speak clearly.

"I'm Andrea," she whispered. "I'm a Superbrain, and I'm practicing."

"That's nice," said the girl. "But see, we have to practice our routines. We have a pep rally tomorrow."

"I didn't know," Andrea whispered.

"Well, now you do," said the girl. She tossed her pompoms on the stage and hopped up. Within moments Andrea was surrounded by jumping girls.

I need to practice, Andrea wanted to say, but couldn't. She rushed off the stage and went straight to Tim's house. It was close to school, and Mr. and Mrs. Barnaby were always so kind and understanding. They would know what to do.

When she burst into the Barnaby home, she found Lenny, Arthur, and Tim studying while gulping down mountains of ice cream covered in various flavors of sauce.

"They won't let me practice!" Andrea said. She sat down at the table and put her head down on her crossed arms.

"Who won't let you practice?" asked Tim.

"The cheerleaders! They have a pep rally tomorrow, and they have to work on their jumps."

"That does it!" stormed Lenny. "I am sick and tired of the attitude that everything the sports teams do is more important than anything at all the Superbrains do."

He rushed out the door, Arthur and Tim hot on his heels.

"Let the boys handle it," Mrs. Barnaby said. "This is their way of taking care of you. Let's walk over. By the time we get there, it will all be worked out."

Andrea walked beside Mrs. Barnaby who pushed Dot in the stroller. The walk was short, but long enough to discuss Mrs. Weathers's order for thirty beetles-in-resin paperweights. Mrs. Barnaby laughed. "I know you think your mom is over the top, but at least she has something useful she enjoys doing. Paperweights are definitely useful items to have."

"I know," Andrea sighed. "I only wish she used beads instead of bugs to decorate."

When they got to the auditorium, they found the cheerleaders standing on the platform glaring down at the three Superbrain boys.

"You've had enough practice," Lenny said.

"We need to be perfect," the cheer captain said.

"But Andrea needs experiencing speaking in front of a large room," said Arthur.

Andrea moved toward the front of the room slowly. She felt foolish that all this fuss was over her timidity before groups. She was just about ready to say "never mind" when a short, dark-haired cheergirl spoke up. "We could take turns," she said.

"Huh?" said the Superbrain boys.

"What I mean is, we could act like we're part of one school instead of like our school is split into the Brains and the Athletes. We'll do a cheer, you clap for us. Then Andrea can do a speech, and we'll be her audience."

"Well—" said Lenny, "there's an idea."

The girls did a cheer that ended with tossed pompoms. Then they sat in the front row of the auditorium while Andrea mounted the steps and stared at them. Her hands trembled.

"It's okay, Andrea," said the dark-haired girl. "You can do it."

Her voice was quiet at first: "Four score and seven years ago our fathers brought forth upon this continent a new nation, conceived in liberty and dedicated to the proposition that all men are created equal."

Great clapping followed the speech and Andrea smiled.

"Our turn," said the captain. The team did a cheer, then Andrea said the next paragraph of the Gettysburg address, and so on, back and forth, until Andrea felt better.

"Thanks," Andrea said. "I feel a lot better now." She rose to go.

"Wait," said the cheerleaders. "We have one more cheer." They girls huddled together on the stage before one shouted, "Give me an A!" the boys replied, "A!"

"Give me an N!"

"Give me an D!"

Andrea realized they were spelling out her name. Her face broke into a smile and tears slid down her cheeks. "Thank you," she whispered.

Afterward, the girl with the short dark hair ran after her.

"Hi, Andrea," she said. "I'm Jenny Mercer."

"I know," said Andrea. "I always wanted to know you, but I'm kind of shy."

The boys came out of the auditorium and joined them. Then Jenny asked, "Tell me again why the Superbrain contest is so important."

There was a great flurry of words, none of which touched on what the team members were thinking. *We're doing this for Miss Thistle so she can die happy.*

Chapter 17

Saturday dawned hot and humid. Tim rushed through breakfast.

"Gotta be at school by seven-thirty. The meet's at ten. Are you guys coming?"

"Of course, we're coming," said his mother, packing strawberry Pop-Tarts into a zippered plastic bag for Tim to take along for a snack. "Do you have your lunch money? Here's ten dollars. Okay, bye, son. I love you."

"Love you too, Mom," Tim shouted as he ran out the door.

The phone rang, and Mrs. Barnaby grabbed it on the first ring. "Oh dear, Arthur, that's terrible. Are you sure? My goodness! Well, you take care of yourself. I'll try to catch Tim."

She slammed the phone down and ran out the front door. "Tim!" she yelled after him. He turned to her but kept moving toward school, walking backward. *No time for primness here*, she thought as she took voice and yelled, "Arthur's sick. He's vomiting. Can't make it. You're on!"

"What?" Tim yelled back. He had stopped but apparently did not want to return home to hear whatever news his mother was yelling.

"He's vomiting!" she yelled. "Sick! He's not coming!"

"Arthur's sick?" Tim yelled.

By now neighbors had cracked open their front doors to see what all the fuss was about. Mrs. Barnaby didn't care. It was all for the Superbrains, all for Judson Christian High and Miss Thistle.

"Yes, he's sick," Mrs. Barnaby shouted. "You're on!"

Satisfied that her son had received the meaning of her shouting, Mrs. Barnaby waved to all the houses in an expansive corporate apology and trotted back into the house to get Dot out of her crib and inform her husband that this would be no ordinary day at the Superbrain meet. Their son, the fearless leader of the Superbrain team and alternate member, Timothy W. Barnaby Jr., would today take his place proudly behind the buzzer to defend the honor of their beloved alma mater.

"All right!" Mr. Barnaby said, pulling his wife close for a celebratory kiss. They got Dot, piled into the van as quickly as possible, and drove off to have breakfast out before heading off for the meet an hour's drive away.

The team breezed through the morning rounds, then met for lunch in the cafeteria of the community college where the meet was being held.

"We did great," said Tim, "but we can't get overly confident. We have to keep ourselves together and not lose our focus."

"Focus is everything," Lenny agreed.

Emma and Andrea toyed with their lettuce-and-tomato salads, until Tim said, "What's the matter?"

"Did you see those kids from Lutton Academy? The suits and ties and matching socks? They could kill us if we meet them in the final round."

"Knock, knock," said Tim, rapping his knuckles on the side of his head. "Hello? Matching socks makes them smarter than us?"

The girls giggled. "No, but it sure makes them look smart."

"Let them look smart," said Lenny. "We'll *be* smart."

"Hey," said Andrea. "Look who's here!"

Arthur's mom led him to their table. He smiled weakly and waved off offers of food with a face twisted in a grimace. "There's no way I can compete today, guys."

"Dude, you look horrible," said Tim.

"Food poisoning," Mrs. Fletcher said, shaking her head. "My fault. Old mayonnaise. At least it's not a serious case."

"Just enough to knock me out of the—uh, Mom—" he said in a semi-panicked manner. Mrs. Fletcher understood his meaning as he rushed away from the table.

Lenny laughed quietly. "Now that's devotion, coming to cheer for your buddies when you're puking out your guts. That's what I call loyalty."

"Me too," said a happy voice. The team looked up to see Jenny Mercer plopping down lightly in an empty chair at their table. "After what you said about this meet, I couldn't stay away. It's great! I'm glad I'm only a junior so I can try out next year!"

"Nope, you can't," said Lenny. He shook his head firmly. "Cheerleaders can't be Superbrains! It's absolutely impossible."

Jenny shot back, "It's not impossible for an overly muscled shot-putting, he-man discus thrower, but it's too much for a black-belt who aced her PSAT, knows the value of pi to twenty-three places, and just so happens to also be a cheerleader? Hmmm?"

Lenny simply stared, wordless.

"Nice buzzer work on that Byzantium question in round three," she offered to Lenny, before walking away.

Emma and Andrea looked at Lenny's gaping mouth and gawking eyes. Then they burst into laughter.

"Okay, this is your fearless leader speaking," said Tim. "Let's pray and get to the next round. There are still two rounds to go, and we want to arrive alive in the last one."

Arrive at the last round they did. Pitted against the feared and matching Lutton Academy, they traded answer for answer until after thirty minutes the score stood tied at sixty-three points each.

The moderator removed his glasses, wiped his face with a handkerchief, polished his glasses, put them back on, and said, "It seems we will go on endlessly with the prepared questions, both teams knowing everything. So I will now exercise my broad discretion and ask a non-practiced general question. We are all very tired. It has been a long day. There will be a slight pause while I confer with the judges on a question to break this tie."

Tim took advantage of the brief respite to breathe deeply and look over the audience. He nudged Andrea on his left when he saw her parents sitting together toward the back. Mrs. Weathers wore a huge feathered hat. She held up a sign that said "Judson Juices

Lutton Lightweights" written in thick black marker. He noticed that Jenny Mercer was sitting dead center grinning, Tim was sure, right at Lenny. Emma's parents were also there, and of course the Barnabys, though Dot was collapsed in a solid nap on her father's shoulder. Most of the audience rustled around as if they were aching for the ordeal to be over.

Miss Thistle, however, seemed completely peaceful. Seated in the front row, she wore a rose-print cotton dress and a beaming smile. She fanned herself in a slow steady rhythm with a folded program of the day's events. Next to her sat Dr. and Mrs. Ross and the four children, then Mr. Garcia with his wife. Three seats further down sat Miss Shore who was clearly not in the least bit happy that the Judson Christian High team had advanced this far.

The moderator resumed his seat.

"Okay, guys, this is it," Tim whispered to his team. He cast a sidelong look at the Lutton Academy team and noticed that they looked as scared as he felt.

"I'd like to thank the audience," intoned the moderator, "for its kind attention. There will be a final discretionary question—not from the manuals—and then you'll be free to go on your way. Everyone ready?"

The eight contestants nodded. Tim sat up tensed and ready, his hand flat on the table, per the rules, ready to bash the buzzer the instant the answer flashed in his brain.

"So here goes. The final question of the West Central Regional Superbrain Meet."

Tim's heart pounded. Sweat trickled down his face.

"What is the name of the collection of data about the countries of the world provided by the Central—"

Tim's hand shot out and pounded the buzzer. When acknowledged, he stated clearly, "The *CIA World Factbook*."

"Judson Christian High wins," said the moderator, bringing his wooden gavel down hard on the podium. "Judson advances to the championships!"

The audience broke into frenzied cheering and applause while the Superbrains high-fived and hugged. Arthur stumbled on his own power up to their table to share the glory of the moment. They shook hands with the Lutton team, then rushed down to the front row to hug Miss Thistle, Dr. Ross, and the Garcias.

"You did it," Miss Thistle said, eyes twinkling with sheer delight. "You're going to state finals!"

Tim walked as if in a fog, his buzzer hand shaking unsteadily. "Look," he said, holding it out, "I can't stop it!"

Everyone looked at the trembling hand and laughed. Tim laughed too.

Arthur bowed to him. "Good you were there instead of me. I didn't know that answer."

"How did you know that?" Emma asked. "I didn't know it either."

Tim shrugged his shoulders and stuffed his shaking hands into his pants pockets. "Oh, it was nothing. I'm just a junior spy, that's all. Spend my summers working in exotic foreign places. No big deal." He lowered his voice, "But don't tell anyone, or I'll have to have you all killed."

Everyone laughed, Andrea most of all, who said, "Tim a spy? That's really funny!" Tim didn't know if he should be happy she was thinking about him in a positive, laughing way or despaired that she was laughing at the idea of his being a spy.

"I will be a great agent," he said. "When my time comes."

"Of course, you will," said Miss Thistle. "Now let's go celebrate."

"Max's Pizza Palace!" Mr. Barnaby shouted. "It's on me. We'll eat pizza, drink root beer, and play ski-ball til they close."

Lenny gave a nice rendition of a Miss Thistle humph. "Yeah," he said. "We'd better celebrate now. We know the school doesn't care."

"What's that supposed to mean?" asked Jenny, easing her way into the conversation as they wandered out to their cars.

"When Dr. Hamilton announced our county win, no one even noticed."

"He announced that?" Andrea asked. "I guess I wasn't listening."

"No one was," said Lenny.

Chapter 18

"We know one thing," said Tim on Monday morning when the team gathered in Miss Thistle's class before school. "There will be a dutiful announcement by Dr. Hamilton over the loudspeaker this morning—"

"And no one will say anything," said Lenny who was feeding himself crumb donuts as usual. "No congratulations."

"But we still won, so it's okay!" said Emma. "Remember, we're not doing this for ourselves. We're doing it for Miss Thistle, and if she's happy, we're happy."

"That's right," said Arthur, his head in a book. "Anything for Miss Thistle, the heartbeat of Judson Christian High School."

"I was thinking about this," said Andrea, "and you know what I realized? I realized that if I never do anything else wonderful and great in all my life, if I help this team do this one thing for Miss Thistle, my life will have really mattered. You know?"

There was silence for a minute, then someone said, "That's cool," and everyone agreed. It really was a great thing to help someone achieve her life's dream.

Tim had walked over to the window and looked out. "Shouldn't people be here by now? It's ten til eight."

Arthur got up and looked out the window while Lenny opened the door and looked down the hall.

"You're right, there's no one around," said Lenny. "Strange."

"I know!" said Arthur. "They all realized the error of their ways, and a holiday was decreed to honor our great regional victory!"

"And everyone heard about it except us. Sounds about right," said Lenny.

"That's what we get for getting here at seven to practice. If we were home listening to the radio in the mornings instead of going over endless sample questions over and over and over and over, we would have heard about the cancellation. Like snow days."

"Those endless sample question goings-over are what got you to the exalted position of regional champion, you know," said Tim.

"Whatever. The point is, where is everyone?"

Emma pulled her phone out of her purse and punched in Jill's number. There was no answer. "Just her voice mail," said Emma. "Which is also weird. She always answers when it's me."

"I'm scared," said Andrea, "Maybe there was a mass kidnapping!"

"Well," said Arthur, "I don't want to say something revolutionary or anything, but how about we go look for them?"

"Ooh, there's an idea," said Lenny, grinning. "Let's go."

Andrea grabbed Tim's arm. Emma grabbed Arthur's. Lenny grabbed Miss Thistle's yard-long wooden pointer from the chalk board rail. They opened the door and looked both ways. The hall was empty.

Every classroom they passed was empty.

"There are cars in the parking lot," Lenny said. "But where are the people?"

"They're in the auditorium," said Lenny. "There's no where else everyone could fit. There must have been an assembly, and we've forgotten about it."

"Then we're late, and we are in a pack of trouble," said Tim. "Just what I need!"

Mr. Garcia was standing outside the auditorium doors. As they approached, he said, "What? The victorious Superbrains themselves are late? Naughty, naughty!" But he was smiling.

As the team members entered the auditorium, someone shouted, "They're here!" The bandmaster counted, "One, two, three, four," and the band burst into a peppy version of the old-fashioned, entirely outdated school song, "Judson, Dear Judson, Great Are Thy Halls." The cheerleaders threw pompoms, and everyone cheered as the Superbrain team members were ushered to the platform. They stood in a line, all smiling broadly and waving (Lenny waved the pointer) while the cheering washed over them, and everyone felt there was nothing bad in the world and never would be again.

Jenny Mercer was in the first row, broadly beaming. Miss Thistle waved a purple Judson pennant their way, herself smiling widely.

When the cheering died away, Dr. Hamilton took the microphone.

"The faculty, staff, and student body of Judson Christian High, gives its deepest congratulations and thanks to the Superbrain team for the honor they have done to our school, and the grace by which they have achieved it."

Loud cheering broke out again. Tim's legs shook. He knew that as the fearless leader of the team it would be up to him to respond. He walked on wobbly legs to the podium and prayed that God would give him the right words to say.

"The Superbrains want to thank the Lord for the opportunity of allowing us to represent our school," he said. "We also want to thank Miss Thistle for her help and dedication to the team." He paused. "And also. We want to thank Dr. Ross, the smartest man in the world, for his great help. And also—" he looked down at Jenny, "thanks for this," he gestured around at the assembly itself. "This is great."

There was endless cheering and stomping of feet. It went on far longer than even the Superbrains could appreciate.

"All right," said Dr. Hamilton. "Some people seem to think that if they cheer all day, there won't be any class!" At which there was more cheering, but Dr. Hamilton raised his hands for quiet. "Good try, freshmen! Now, let's get back to class."

That afternoon a special "Tribute To Our Superbrains" edition of the school paper was published with a poem titled "Our

Five Magi," written by the upcoming valedictorian, Jaycie McPhail.

> *They drip with knowledge,*
> *Pour out wisdom,*
> *A superb rain on our heads*

Lenny scoffed at the Superb Rain/Superbrain poem.

"What does it mean?" he demanded. "And why is it spaced so weirdly on the page?"

Arthur declared that it was art, that it didn't have to mean anything, that poems didn't have to line up, and didn't need periods at the end.

"If I can't hold the distinction of being the valedictorian of the senior class, I can at least be compared to a magnificent precipitation by the woman who is going to have that exalted position."

Lenny hit him on the head with a book, and Arthur returned the favor.

Chapter 19

Sunday night Tim lay in bed and stared up at the ceiling. Uncertainty, elation, fleeting determination, and outright fear jumbled up his thoughts.

It had started a few hours earlier. Andrea had called him just after dinner. She had an idea and wanted Tim's feedback. As Tim listened to her, a pinpoint of queasiness in his gut grew into a solid block of anxiety.

He knew Andrea would be unable to galvanize the group into action although the idea had been hers. If it was going to be done, he himself would have to do it.

The risk was tremendous; the outcome uncertain.

Tim slid out of bed and knocked on his parents' door.

"Dad, Mom," he called softly.

"Come in," they answered.

Tim sat at the end of their bed. He bowed his head and stared at his folded hands.

"What if you learn there's something you could do that might help someone, but you don't want to do it?" he began.

"Why don't you want to do it?" his father asked. Mr. Barnaby sat up in bed and turned on the bedside lamp.

"I would have to give up something important. A lot of people would be disappointed, maybe angry." Tim looked up at his parents. "Plus, it might not help the person. It might make things worse."

Mrs. Barnaby sat up in bed and looked at her firstborn. Pain and indecision were written on his face. "But, best-case scenario—if it did work—would the help you could offer do a lot of good?" she asked.

Tim saw his parents exchange a questioning glance. He knew they wanted to know the particulars, but he also knew they would not probe for details. They would trust him to say what he needed to say.

"It could save someone's life," said Tim, staring at his parents' bedspread.

"Well, then," said his father. "That's that."

Mr. Barnaby snapped off the bedside lamp and slid back down under the covers.

Tim sat there a long moment longer. He sighed, heaved himself off his parents' bed, and walked shakily out of the room.

"Thanks, guys," he said as he softly shut their door.

He made a few phone calls.

Emma said, "Yeah, duh!"

Lenny said, "Best idea you ever had, Barnaby!"

Arthur said, "Capital concept, Tim. I'm in."

Andrea said, "Thanks, Tim. You're great."

And Jenny Mercer, fresh from her triumph of orchestrating the impromptu Superbrain pep rally, added the icing on the cake that made it all so very simple.

Tim went to bed again. He thanked the Lord for how far the team had come. *Give us strength to do what's right*, he prayed before drifting off to sleep.

Chapter 20

In the morning, meeting for their usual practice session, Tim took the pulse of the team again.

"Are we together? It has to be one hundred percent," he said. "If anyone wavers, it won't work."

Emma and Andrea both wore looks of fierce determination.

"We're not budging," Emma said.

"Not an inch," said Andrea. "Not a millimeter."

The door opened and Jenny came in. She nodded to everyone with a smile and a thumbs-up. "We're good," she said.

Arthur cleared his throat. "We all realize, of course, that if she doesn't go for this, all our work is wasted, and we're dead in the water."

"If she doesn't go for it, she's dead in the ground," said Lenny.

So they sat and waited for her.

When Miss Thistle entered her room that morning, she saw the team sitting straight and quiet, simply staring at her. Also in the room was Jenny Mercer, one of the varsity cheerleaders and a very good ninth-grade geography student a few years back.

"Hello, my friends!" Miss Thistle gushed. "What a weekend. I haven't had so much pizza in years. I don't believe I've actually ever had root beer in my life either. Daddy was always so careful to avoid anything that smacked of worldliness, and you know the word *beer*—"

She stopped. Something strange had subdued her group of normally noisy team members.

"What is it?" she said.

Tim stood. "We have a proposition for you, Miss Thistle," he said.

"Yes?"

"But you need to sit down while we explain it," said Emma. "Because you might get upset."

"Yes, good idea," said Arthur. Lenny said nothing, nor did he eat donuts. Andrea stared at the floor. Jenny fiddled with something in her purse.

Miss Thistle settled herself into her chair. "All right," she said. "I'm ready to be upset."

Tim, who had remained standing, got right to the point. "You want us to win the Superbrain championship."

"With all my heart."

Tim swallowed hard. *Here it comes.* He noticed squirming in seats, though he knew each heart was settled.

"And we—with all our hearts—want you to beat your cancer. We want you to get the whole treatment: surgery, radiation, chemo, whatever it takes. We want you to try to live."

And then it was silent.

"So you know," said Miss Thistle. "How—"

"It's my fault," said Tim. "You remember the night we all met at your house, ate pie, and decided to quit the team and go back to our regular lives?"

Miss Thistle nodded. "Of course."

"Well, the next morning, we got here early to write you a thank-you note, but no one had a pen. I'm sorry to admit that I rummaged through your top drawer to find one, and I saw the paper. I snooped—no excuses—and here we are."

"The morning my desk drawer was not firmly closed. I remember."

"Since we read the note, we know about the cancer," said Arthur.

"I've lived sixty-one years," said Miss Thistle. "Not quite the three score and ten, but more than many people get and—"

"We need you," said Tim. Here he actually stomped his foot, then blushed at his firmness. He took a deep breath.

"We the Superbrains have agreed. If you won't get treatment, we all quit the team. We forfeit our regional victory, and we don't go to finals. But if you do get treatment, we'll do our best to win this thing. We know the finals are harder than the other meets, but we are prepared to do our all-out, absolute, one-thousand-percent best."

Miss Thistle stared at Tim. "You can't do this to me." She shook her head. "You have to go to finals. But I will not see Thaddeus with my hair all fallen out!"

Miss Thistle clapped her hand over her mouth and looked from one astonished face to the next. *Oh dear*, she thought, *what will I say next to these children? What can I say that they will understand?*

She remembered the looks she had seen on Tim's and Andrea's faces when they laughed with each other. She remembered how she herself had felt things when she was only eighteen and then nineteen—hardly any older than these children here.

"All right," she said. "Here's the truth. You know that Dr. Greenleaf, the president of South U, will be presiding over the final Superbrains competition."

"Of course," said Tim.

"And you girls know about the boy I was once engaged to."

"Yes," said Andrea.

Miss Thistle paused, tilted her head to one side, and said, "Thaddeus Greenleaf was that boy."

The room grew silent. No one moved. "I know, I know," Miss Thistle said, smiling. "It's unbelievable. But I haven't seen him since he walked away from me long ago, and I'd like to look— well—pretty, when I see him again."

There was an awkward pause, and then Andrea asked, "What happened, Miss Thistle? I mean to the engagement?"

"It's a long story," said Miss Thistle, "and not my finest hour, I don't think, though it turned out to be his." Her voice drifted off to a whisper.

"Will you tell us?" asked Emma, who then added quickly, "You don't have to."

"My goodness, of course, she doesn't have to!" said Jenny. "It's personal."

"It certainly is," said Miss Thistle. "But here goes: When I was nineteen years old, I started teaching in a school in the basement of the Baptist church. It was called Adoniram Judson High after the great American missionary from way back when. Yes, this very school, but then, as I say, it was in the church basement. The government wasn't doing a lot for the education of colored folks at that time—back when we were called *colored folks.*"

Miss Thistle smiled and looked at the teenagers. As they all appeared interested, she continued.

"My parents had sacrificed enough for me to attend Judson myself for two years. I graduated at seventeen and went on to complete one year at the junior college. Then the money ran out, and I had to quit with only one year of college under my belt. I wanted to finish college, but the opportunity did not arise again.

"So I taught at Judson. I worked my students hard! Education was the ticket out of poverty, which of course continues to be the case. Slackers don't go far, and I didn't put up with them. I was perhaps not as gentle with students then as I am now. I was fiercely determined they would succeed! If I couldn't go to college, I was determined my students would go.

"Now, I was only nineteen, but qualified teachers were scarce, so I taught all the English classes, ninth through twelfth grades. There was a big senior boy that year, nineteen years old, and the handsomest boy I had ever seen."

"He was your same age." Emma whispered.

"He had the finest mind of any person I had ever known. Of course, I was the teacher and he was my student!"

Emma and Andrea both sniffed and grabbed tissues.

"My heart finally gave way when I found out that he liked me too. I knew this would not be good for the school, so I quit teaching, so we could start seeing each other."

"You quit?"

Miss Thistle nodded. "I had a very finely tuned conscience then as I do today, being one of the Lord's own children as I am," she said. "I could not in good conscience continue teaching a boy I had fallen in love with, and I was determined he would not have to stop his education. So I stopped teaching. I confided in my pastor who understood, and I went to work in the grocery store. The pastor took over my teaching duties, and Thaddeus finished up his senior year."

"While you worked at the grocery store, you got engaged to him."

"I did," Miss Thistle said. She smiled.

The boys looked away, but the girls giggled.

"What happened?" asked Andrea.

"What happened was he decided not to go to college."

"That's it?" said Tim.

"That's it! He said he wanted to marry me right away. He didn't care about college. He wanted to work at the grocery store with me, settle down, and raise a few children. Maybe farm a few acres on the side."

"And this made you mad," said Lenny.

"It made me *fiery* mad," said Miss Thistle. "I would happily have waited until he graduated from college—he had such a future ahead of him, but no, he said, it was now or never! He'd marry me right after he graduated from high school, or he wouldn't marry me at all."

Miss Thistle paused before going on. "I begged him to reconsider. You may not be able to understand this today when almost anyone can go to college, but back then education meant everything, and here was a boy whose intellect made so many things possible. He could have succeeded in a great way."

"So you broke up with him," said Emma.

"Not at first. I tried to reason with him. I even yelled," Miss Thistle said. "Then, as now, there was a lack of recognized, identified, brilliantly positioned African-American men. He could have easily been an attorney or an eminent surgeon or president of the United States, and he was aspiring to run a store and snag himself a school teacher! It was a crime.

"I wept when he walked across the stage at graduation because I knew it meant the end of our engagement. I even knew that I would throw myself into teaching for the rest of my life (sometimes you just know these things), but I didn't care. Right there and then in the audience at that graduation, I wrote him a note. Even though I loved him very deeply, I tore into that young man. I called him a slacker, a disgrace.

"After the ceremony, he walked right up to me, and he said, 'Let's get married next Saturday,' and I said, 'No, Thaddeus, you need to go to college,' and I handed him the note.

"He read it right there in front of me. I took the engagement ring off my finger and handed it to him. He stared at me a few moments and then turned and left. I haven't seen him since. And when I do see him again—now that he has made something of himself—I want to look pretty, not emaciated and bald from chemotherapy!"

"I cannot believe you scolded the famous Dr. Greenleaf!" said Andrea.

"I did," Miss Thistle shook her head, wiped her eyes, and stared at the ground. "And now look where he is."

"Did you know that Thaddeus Greenleaf was the first African-American from this town to receive a Doctor of Philosophy degree?" Arthur asked. "I read that somewhere."

"Thaddeus Greenleaf," said Miss Thistle. "was the first *person* from *this county* to earn a PhD."

"He might still like you," said Arthur. "You know he never married."

"How do you know that?" asked Lenny.

"Google, dummy," said Arthur. "I Googled him after Miss Thistle mentioned him during that first assembly."

Miss Thistle coughed. "Never mind that. Yes, I want to see him again, but more importantly you must see the fulfillment of all your work. There can be no discussion of your quitting for any reason."

"We have worked hard," said Emma, and Tim saw her wavering.

"It would be so nice for us to win while he's there," said Andrea, and Tim saw where this wavering was going: *She's going to die anyway; let's give her this chance to see her old flame while she's still healthy.*

Then his brain clicked on.

"No, ma'am," Tim said. "We do not have to. We made a pact among ourselves, and we will not change our minds. What good is it to anyone if you see this man and then die? We want you to live. We stand by our proposal: You get treatment; we study. You don't; we forfeit."

"Isn't that a bit forceful?" she said. Her eyebrows arched and her voice was clipped.

Lenny stood up. "Yes, ma'am, it is, and maybe we're wrong." He looked around for support, found it, and continued. "Maybe it's even mean. Maybe you have firmly and finally decided against treatment. But maybe you're not sure. Maybe you could be convinced to try to save your life. This contest is the only leverage we have. Miss Thistle, we want you to live."

Miss Thistle coughed and moved about in her chair to get more comfortable. "I am already past sixty. Many people die in their sixties."

"Or you may live to be over one hundred," said Tim. "You won't know if you don't try."

Miss Thistle stared from face to face, finally settling on Jenny. "And what, may I ask, is the significance of Miss Mercer's being here this morning? I am guessing she did not randomly stop by."

Jenny grinned. "Dr. Milton Jones is my stepfather, Miss Thistle. It's okay, most people don't know. He married my mother when I was very small, and he has always been my daddy."

"The eminent oncologist," said Miss Thistle.

"Yes. He's really good. He and I talked over the weekend, and he has agreed to bear the expense of your treatment."

"The expense?"

"Every cent."

Miss Thistle looked around at these children, her team. How much she wanted to see Thaddeus, and now she could only do so if she agreed to undergo the rigors, pain, and sickness of surgery, maybe radiation, probably chemotherapy. *Drip, drip, drip.* Potent, nasty, dreadful medicines through an IV into an already sick body, making it sicker before it made you better, maybe not helping, all the while making you bald and skinny!

Then again, how good did she look as it was, falling apart with fatigue, using a cane to steady herself? Vanity, the Preacher said, all is vanity!

"Miss Thistle," said Tim, "We love you."

The others nodded, and Miss Thistle suddenly saw from their perspective. She was a little old lady they loved, and for whom they were willing to forego an opportunity of great praise. They were moths flying away from the flame to help her. She nodded. The precious gift of motivation had been lovingly laid at her feet.

"I'll call Dr. Jones this afternoon," she said.

"Now," said Jenny. She spoke into her cell phone. "Here she is, Dad. We got her!" She handed the phone to Miss Thistle.

Chapter 21

"There you are!" shouted Milton Jones. He was tall, lean, and bespectacled. "I've been waiting for you. It's Miss Thistle, everyone's favorite teacher. I've heard all about you. The kids adore you. Let me see, Preston Phillips sent over your file . . . here it is, you've got a bit of a problem with a tumor, but nothing we can't get to, Lord willing, if we get right on it. Surgery in the morning, yes?"

"As in tomorrow morning?" breathed Miss Thistle. "Why, I haven't even set these old bones down in your nice leather chair here yet, Dr. Jones."

"Milton! Call me Milton. Yes, yes, tomorrow, why wait? We've waited long enough. Nothing more to eat today! Sit! Sit! Don't drink anything after midnight."

Miss Thistle sat and listened.

"After you're all sewn up and rarin' to go, then we start on the state-of-the-art treatment modalities. We draw lines on you with black marker and zap you with a little radiation. Then, later, if you need it, we blast you with some nasty medicines we have the nerve to call chemotherapy."

"Your daughter Jenny was under the impression that the costs—"

Dr. Jones chuckled. "Don't you worry about that, Miss Thistle." He straightened his tie and winked at her. "I've got plenty of money. What else should I do with it but help Judson's favorite teacher?"

Miss Thistle's eyes twinkled. "All right, Dr. Jones. I guess that's that." She took a deep breath and exhaled. "I guess we should talk about the treatment then."

"You'll vomit. You'll lose weight. You'll feel awful . . ." He said this happily as someone who was suggesting an afternoon's nature walk. With such a doctor, a person would either run away quickly or be devoted to him. Miss Thistle was instantly devoted.

Still, she pressed the matter of her age one more time. "I am already sixty-one."

"I'm forty-three, nice to meet you," said the doctor holding out his hand in this oldest of stale jokes. He laughed. "You're valuable, Miss Thistle. The kids love you. From what I understand, if you don't give living the old college try, they are all quitting the team. You quit; they quit. Seems fair and square to me."

Miss Thistle opined that perhaps a woman longing for another blue sky and great lungsful of fresh air might be presuming on the grace and timing of God.

"Don't go there, Miss Thistle," said Dr. Jones. "God made the world to be enjoyed. He wants you to love the blue sky. Blue sky was His idea."

On her way out the door, brochures and folders and treatment schedules in hand, Miss Thistle smiled. "Thank you, Milton. I appreciate your attitude. I'll try hard to pay you back. Truly I will."

"Truly you won't, you silly goose! I told you, I can't think of anything I need your money for. Besides, you don't have any. Bake me some pies. That'll do!"

"That I will do, Milton," said Miss Thistle. "If I don't make a good chocolate cream pie, I don't know who does!"

He walked her all the way out to her car and opened the door for her. As she settled down into her seat and turned the ignition, she said aloud, "Well, here we go."

Chapter 22

"You did what?" said Mrs. Barnaby. She stopped dead with a casserole in her hands, midway between the stove and the table.

"We told her we'd quit if she didn't get treatment for her cancer."

"I knew it," said Mrs. Barnaby. "I knew she was sick."

Ike sat on the floor next to him, banging his tail against the chair leg. Dot whacked her spoon on her highchair tray.

"Quit, as in throw away your regional win, give up your chance at winning the state championship, toss off your one and only opportunity to pour glory over Judson Christian High and this entire little town?" Mr. Barnaby's voice was stern, unbending.

"Yes, sir." Tim hung his head.

"Did it occur to you that this is her choice, that she is a grown woman, that the decision to undergo painful, possibly ineffective treatment should be left to the person getting that treatment?"

"Yes, sir." Tim's head hung lower, almost touching his empty plate.

"So that the possible outcomes are: First, she says, no. You quit; she dies. No one is happy.

"Second, she says yes, does all the horrible treatment, and still dies, thus adding agonies to her final months, basically of your infliction because you almost forced her."

Tim stared at his plate, hardly breathing.

"Third, she says yes, does all the horrible treatment, and then recovers. You having maybe won or maybe lost the finals."

"Thus saving her life," said Mrs. Barnaby softly.

Tim nodded. "Yes," he breathed. His heart felt heavy within his chest as he wondered how he had been so horribly foolish, so badly misled. None of the possibilities now seemed right.

Mr. Barnaby turned to his wife and said, "Our son led a group of teenagers in throwing away their one chance at greatness to pressure their teacher into getting treatment that might save her life."

"I know," Mrs. Barnaby said. "It's the most wonderful thing he has ever done."

Tim looked up to see his parents beaming at him. "Proud of you, son," Mr. Barnaby said. "And I've got to say, I'm glad she said yes. I would've hated for you kids to miss your big chance. That was quite a risk you took."

Tim nodded his head. "Thanks, guys," he said.

His mother put down the casserole and hugged Tim. "I don't know if you were right. It's hard to say. And of course, she can always change her mind or stop the treatment if it gets too awful. But it was extraordinarily giving of you guys."

An hour later, the Barnabys loaded up in the van to go to the mall. Mrs. Barnaby decided she needed a new dress to wear to the championships, and Mr. Barnaby believed one of the best things he could do for his wife's happiness was to accompany her to the stores to assure her as she appeared from the dressing room that each dress was flattering and did not, in fact, make her look fat.

Tim, of course, did not relish the idea of sitting in a "husband's chair" outside the ladies dressing room waiting for his mother to model a series of dresses. Happily, his parents agreed to pick up Lenny on the way. Tim and Lenny left Mr. and Mrs. Barnaby and Dot at Sears and headed straight to the food court where they intended to discover how many orders of french fries could be eaten by the ordinary teenaged boy in an hour.

It appeared the answer to that question was going to be "in excess of eleven large orders" when an all-too familiar voice interrupted their eating.

"So, this time it's you pressuring her instead of the other way round."

The boys stopped chewing, though their mouths were full, and looked up into the face of Miss Bethany Shore.

"Word travels," said Lenny, his mouth full of food.

"It sure does," she replied. "Everyone thinks you've pulled a rabbit out of a hat—made the old lady do something no one else could ever have gotten her to do."

Miss Shore sat in an empty chair beside Tim. She leaned in. "The truth is you know you can't win. Isn't that right?" She smiled and nodded at them. "And here's a great way for you to get out of a pickle with your honor intact."

She leaned back in her chair and laughed. "You couldn't beat the big schools at the state tournament, but you don't want to be humiliated, so you've designed the perfect scenario. You know Miss Thistle doesn't want to get treatment. If she'd wanted to get treatment, she would have already done so. She won't get the treatment, and you can still be heroes. It's priceless, really."

Lenny looked from Tim to Miss Shore. Then he said, "Why is this so important to you, Miss Shore?"

"Yeah," said Tim. "Why do you even care whether we compete? Why do you hate us?"

Miss Shore laughed. "It's not you, silly boy. It's your school. It's Maggie Thistle."

"You hate Miss Thistle?" said Tim, staring. "How can anyone hate Miss Thistle?"

Miss Shore stood. "You try working as hard as I have and being passed over for a little old unqualified nobody. Try that for a while and then tell me you're not mad."

Miss Shore strode off into the mall crowd.

"Wow," said Lenny. "She's really ticked off."

"She's jealous of how much we all love Miss Thistle," said Tim. "And she's madder now that she knows we're willing to give up everything for Miss Thistle to have a chance to get well."

"No one's ever been that nice to Miss Shore," said Lenny.

There was a long pause before Tim said, "Maybe we should try it."

Lenny nodded. "It can't hurt."

Chapter 23

It was cold at three in the morning when the team gathered at the Barnabys' house for donuts and hot chocolate before heading out on the five hour drive down to South University.

Early as it was, no one was at all tired. According to Miss Thistle's instructions, everyone had gone to bed at eight o'clock, slept until one, then got ready for the long ride. Hopefully they would get some sleep on the way.

"Absurd to be up at this time," said Mr. Barnaby. "We should have gone down last night and stayed in a motel!"

"Think of the expense of that," his wife chided him gently. "This saves a lot of money. Besides it's fun."

"Fun for you! You'll be sleeping like a baby—with the baby—all the way down while I try to keep my eyelids propped open with toothpicks!"

Everyone laughed. Headlights came down the street at last, and the Rosses and Miss Thistle came into the house. Miss Thistle wore her prettiest pink dress, and she was shining with excitement. "I've never looked forward to a day in my life as much as I am looking forward to this one," she said.

"You are looking surprisingly well, Miss Thistle," said Mr. Barnaby. "From what I heard through the grapevine you were supposed to be nothing but bald bones. You look great!"

"I convinced Dr. Jones to wait until tomorrow to make me bald and sick," she said with a little laugh. "But let's not talk about that."

"Certainly not," said Mrs. Barnaby. She collected the cocoa cups, diapered Dot, washed her hands, and tidied up while the team gathered in a circle to pray over the day.

Dr. Ross prayed. "Father, we give thanks for this extraordinary day you have brought us to. We ask—"

He was interrupted by a gasping, choking sound. Eyes flew open around the prayer circle as Miss Thistle fell. Her head banged sickeningly on the hardwood floor. Emma and Andrea both screamed.

Mr. Barnaby called 911, and Dr. Ross knelt by Miss Thistle to check for heartbeat and respiration.

"Pulse is fast," he said. "Breathing is labored."

Mr. Barnaby repeated this into the phone. "They're coming," he said.

Minutes later, EMTs rushed into the house. Miss Thistle's inert form was surrounded by the medical professionals while everyone else backed away and prayed silently.

"We're going to go ahead and transport her to the hospital," the EMT said.

The medics gently placed the unconscious Miss Thistle on a gurney and wheeled her out to the ambulance.

"I'm going too," said Dr. Ross.

"Of course," said his wife. "I'll take the children home. We'll wait to hear from you there."

The Rosses rushed out the door.

The teenagers seemed suddenly lost. Neither Miss Thistle nor Dr. Ross would accompany them to the final tournament.

"What are we going to do now?" Arthur asked.

Tim hesitated for only an instant before saying, "We are going to South University. We are going to win the championship. We'll get a picture of all of us with Dr. Greenleaf, and we'll bring home the trophy. That's what we're going to do!"

"What are we waiting for?" said Mr. Barnaby. "Get in the van everyone. We've got places to go and people to see!"

Mr. and Mrs. Barnaby packed Dot into her car seat and then loaded everyone else up. Coolers of soda pop and snacks came next. The lunch hamper. A final prayer was offered to the Lord, and the van moved off down the road.

They passed the small general hospital on the way out of town. The ambulance was parked in the emergency area, lights still flashing.

"God be with you," said Janet Barnaby.

Amens drifted up from the back seats.

Chapter 24

South University spread its dozens of stately brick buildings over several hundred perfectly maintained acres. Wide lawns dotted with ancient oaks fronted each building. Azaleas splashed red and purple and white in wide swaths. Tulips stood in ranks and files of every possible color, and wisteria cascaded purple over power lines, trees, and lattices.

The Superbrains from Judson Christian High realized their insignificance as they threaded their way through the noisy mass of big-school academics. Everywhere they looked everyone else seemed bigger, taller, smarter, better dressed.

"Remember, we're as good as anybody here," said Arthur. "They won their regional meets; we won ours."

"We have a little region," said Andrea.

"But we have a big purpose," said Tim. "Don't let these guys scare you. They have fancy clothes, briefcases, and laptops. Who needs that stuff? We're prepared."

They entered a large building on which hung a large banner that read: *Welcome, Superbrains!*

Inside they found a line of tables set up for team registrations, found the correct table, and stood in line.

They talked about the day's agenda while waiting their turn to register. Befitting academic precision, it would be an efficient tournament. The first round would start at nine-thirty: all sixteen regional champion teams in eight separate matches. Of course, eight teams would be eliminated. The second round would start at ten-thirty with the eight remaining teams in four different rooms. At eleven-thirty the four remaining teams would face each other in two semifinal matches. Then there would be a break for lunch. At two o'clock, the final match between the last two teams would take place in the main auditorium.

"Mornin'," said the lady when it was their turn. She had very orange hair with a full inch of white roots, and she wore extremely red lipstick. A white sticker affixed to her yellow blouse proclaimed her to be Mrs. Melva Lemon. A coffee mug with the red lipstick clearly smacked on it sat next to her fat arm on the table. "How you kids doin' this fine day? You here to win the championship?"

"Yes, ma'am," said Tim, "We're the team from Judson Christian High, West Central Region champs."

The lady spun in her chair to face her laptop computer, tapped away for a minute on the keyboard, then said, "All right, that's the team of Barnaby, Bryce, Fletcher, Luther, and Weathers."

"Yes," said Tim, "but the Barnaby—that's me—is only the alternate."

"No alternates at Finals," said the lady. She took a long sip of her coffee. "Everyone competes, five to a team. New rule this year. I thought everyone had that."

"Uh, no," said Tim. "We didn't get that one."

"Lost in the mail probably," said the lady. "Never mind; doesn't matter. Everyone gets to play in the finals. Makes it nice for all the parents who come such a long way. Who's your sponsor? I see, it's Thistle. Where's Mr. Thistle?"

"*Miss* Thistle, but she's not here. She's in the hospital," said Arthur, pushing his way through to speak to the orange-haired lady. "She had some kind of attack this morning, and we had to come without her."

"My goodness! I hope that's not a problem," said the lady. "I wonder . . ." A whirring noise interrupted her, and she turned to the printer. She grabbed the sheet of paper as it slid out. "Here's your room assignment for the first round. Good luck."

She reached for a blue binder and flipped through it as the team said thank you and began to walk toward their assigned room.

The first round was an easy win for the Judson team. They faced a team from an all-boys military school too full of inflated self-esteems to be able to focus on the task at hand. The round went so quickly that there was time before the second round to look around at some of the many displays scattered around the hall. Arthur and Lenny both spoke with the Air Force and Marine Corps recruiters, each of whom attempted to excel the other in praise of his particular branch of service.

The girls sat in armchairs with cans of diet soda and talked excitedly about the cuteness factor achieved by each of the boys on the disappointed team they had so recently eliminated. But when two of those young men actually approached with the desire to speak with them, Andrea and Emma dissolved into shrieks of nervous giggles until the boys went away.

Tim stood to the side observing all of this, worrying about Miss Thistle, wishing Dr. Ross were there, and hoping Miss Shore had stayed at home.

She hadn't, and she sat front and center at their second round.

"Don't look at her," Tim commanded the team. "Keep your eyes on the judges, the moderator, or the buzzer. Study your hands. Don't look at her. She's going to try to distract you with some look."

"But why?" Andrea asked.

"She's just an angry person." said Arthur.

"She's lost her way," said Lenny. "Let's be nice."

"Be nice, yes, but let's do what we came to do: win for Miss Thistle," said Tim. "Concentrate. Quick hands, clear answers. That's it."

They made quick work of their second opponent.

There was great back-slapping and general congratulations in the hall after that round as the parents descended on their success-ful children.

"We'd love to talk," Tim said, "but we have to stay focused. Is there any news on Miss Thistle?"

"She's resting," said Mr. Barnaby. "The doctor says it's anemia, dehydration, stress, general weakness from her illness and recent surgery. Nothing life-threatening, but enough to knock her off her feet for a day or two. She'll be fine. You kids get this work done. Blast them to the moon!"

"We'll do our best," they said.

As the kids walked purposefully down the hall to their semifinal match, Mr. Barnaby sighed and said to all the parents, "Don't tell the kids, but Ross says when she gained consciousness and realized she was missing the championships, Miss Thistle broke down and cried. They finally gave her something to make her sleep."

The room filled up quickly to see the semifinal match between Judson Christian High and Boone High, the largest high school in the state. The Boone administration had been able to pick from over a thousand seniors. As the Judson team held hands in a prayer circle prior to seating themselves behind the table, Tim felt Andrea's hand trembling. The Boone kids had big brains, big bodies, and mountains of confidence. Their school was used to winning everything from football championships to West Point appointments.

"We know everything in those books," Tim said, fearlessly leading. "All we have to do is listen to the question, smack the buzzer, say the answer. One, two, three easy steps. Now let's pray."

Each boy prayed short supplications for recall, quickness, and clarity.

"Praying, are you?" said a familiar voice.

"Yes, ma'am," said Lenny, nodding at Miss Shore. "Have a nice day, Miss Shore."

She walked off slowly.

Question, buzzer, answer. Question, buzzer, answer. Back and forth for the next thirty minutes. Then the Boone High team made a spectacular mistake—announcing that the capital of Australia was Sydney. The incorrect Boone team member swore loudly at his error, and a judge rang a bell.

"Minus one point for inappropriate language per rule fifteen," the judge intoned.

The largest of the Boone team members rose from his seat. He towered well in excess of six feet.

"What?" he bellowed.

"Don't look," said Tim quietly to his team. "Don't get involved; don't take sides. Just sit and wait. Focus. Listen carefully, smack fast, answer clearly. One, two, three."

Tim's advice was good. The Boone team struggled to recover from the penalty point and were unable to because of their emotional distraction. Judson stayed focused, missed only one of the next ten questions, and were eight ahead at the end of the round.

"Judson advances to the final round," shouted the moderator.

Tim heaved an enormous sigh of relief, fell back in his chair, then noticed his hands were shaking and a tear was running down his face. They all broke into smiles and laughter. Everyone hugged everyone.

"Lunch!" shouted Mr. Barnaby. "You need a good lunch now! Not too much though. You don't want to be stuffed and thinking about your stomachs at two o'clock this afternoon."

"I can't eat," said Andrea.

"Me either," said Emma.

"Oh, you are eating," said Mrs. Barnaby. "Trust me on this one. I know. Girls think they can go without eating, but then you won't be able to think! We need thinking girls, so we need eating girls."

They ate out on the lawn. Mr. Barnaby ran into the snack shop twice for more bags of potato chips and cookies. People came over to congratulate them and wish them well.

"Here comes Miss Shore," said Arthur. "Remember what we talked about on the ride down? Like Tim said, even if she can't be nice to us, we can be nice to her."

She came. "Well, you've done it." She tossed her long blonde hair over her shoulder. "You've made it to the state finals. Where's our reverend holy mother who can do no wrong?"

"She's in the hospital, Miss Shore," Tim said, "but we're glad you could make it. Thanks for coming."

Miss Shore looked startled and seemed unable to speak for a moment. "Is she dying of that chemo you kids made her take? Is that it?"

"No, she's just a little tired," Arthur said. The girls nodded and tried to look at Miss Shore happily.

"So you left her in the hospital and came on down here to make fools of yourselves against the big teams . . ." Miss Shore's voice drifted off as she realized that so far Judson had done the exact opposite of embarrassing themselves.

Lenny wiped his hands on his pants, got up from the blanket, and walked over to the former Judson Christian High faculty member.

"Miss Shore, I know you don't want us to win this competition. That's your prerogative. You can root for whomever you want to root for, but we want you to know that we all want the best for you, and we hope you find a lot of happiness in your life."

He tossed his crumpled trash into a trash can, smiled at Miss Shore, and sat back down with the team.

Miss Shore stared at the team for a few moments with a surprised expression before walking away.

"She's not any stranger than my mom," said Andrea.

"She's just sad," said Emma. "You can tell if you look. Lenny was right. We just need to be kind to her."

Mr. Barnaby cleared his throat loudly. "You're right about that for sure, but right now you need to concentrate on winning the Superbrains trophy for Miss Thistle. It's time to blast off for the stars!"

Chapter 25

"Ladies and gentlemen," said the orange-haired lady the Judson team had met earlier that day. "My name is Melva Lemon, and I am president of the State Teachers' Association."

There was a great deal of applause for Mrs. Lemon, who appeared to savor each clap.

"It is my great honor to welcome you to the championship round of this year's Superbrains competition!"

More cheering and even some stomping of feet followed this statement.

"And I am deeply honored to have the privilege of introducing our moderator for this final round. Ladies and gentlemen, please welcome a man we all know and admire, the president of this great university, Dr. Thaddeus Greenleaf!"

Great applause and tremendous cheering arose from the audience as Dr. Greenleaf came out from backstage. He was a large black man, still very handsome at sixty-one. He shook hands with Mrs. Lemon, who cast a worried look toward the Judson table before rushing down the stage steps to her front-row seat.

"Thank you," he said. "It is certainly my privilege to see these accomplished students. Let's meet them now."

He read the name of each student, first the Judson team, each of whom walked out from behind the curtain and took his place behind his chair at the Judson table. Then he introduced the five young ladies who represented the team from Martha Washington Academy.

Martha Washington had won this competition before, but not in a number of years. The five MWA girls were quiet, well-mannered, and focused.

"Don't let their focus ruin your focus," said Tim.

"They have the cutest uniforms!" said Emma, and Andrea agreed.

"Girls," said Arthur, "you can admire their clothes later. Right now let's focus on the questions."

It began. Dr. Greenleaf read the questions, buzzers were buzzed, clear answers given, points awarded.

Martha Washington gained an early lead. Judson gained, drew ahead, fell back. Score tied. One of the Washington girls began to cough. The attack grew so violent, the girl had to excuse herself. A short recess was taken while she got water and calmed down.

"I'm sorry," she said quietly, then proceeded to answer three questions in a row.

Who was the president of Mexico in 1930? In what year was the United States removed from the gold standard? Which element is number forty-five on the periodic table? In which state is the most coal mined? Who was the first Asian-American astronaut? Which religious leader's preaching sparked a revival in Wales? What is Canada's highest point?

And so forth. Tim made the mistake of looking at the audience during a brief pause caused by Dr. Greenleaf's needing a drink of water. Looking down at the front row, he saw Mrs. Lemon chatting with Miss Shore. There was a worried look on Mrs. Lemon's face, and a decidedly joyous look on Miss Shore's.

"She looks awfully happy," Tim said. "Maybe we won her over with our kindness at lunch time."

"That would be so great," said Lenny.

"Focus, guys," said Andrea. "Listen, smack, answer."

What is the distance to Alpha Centauri? What is the length of Saturn's day? How many people fit in Shea Stadium? Who won the 1958 World Series? By how many electoral votes did

Richard Nixon win the presidency in 1968? Who was Secretary of the Interior under Gerald Ford? In which state is the most corn grown?

Dr. Greenleaf's voice boomed. "The score is tied, ninety-five to ninety-five. This is our final question."

Focus.

Listen, smack the buzzer, answer.

One, two, three.

"Aside from the ice caps, name the two coldest biomes on earth."

Tim smashed his buzzer. "Tundra and taiga."

"Correct," boomed Dr. Greenleaf. "Judson Christian High wins!"

The noise of cheering was so great and the shaking by his teammates so exuberant, Tim could hardly stay in his chair. In fact, he did not but slid out onto the floor. He managed with great effort to get back up, and then the whole team walked over to the Martha Washington girls and shook hands warmly. The runners-up were gracious and congratulatory.

"We get a trip to Disney World either way, so we're happy," one of the girls said.

"Wow," said Andrea. "I want to go to your school!"

"No, you don't," said Tim. "I mean, maybe you do, but you can't because you have to stay with me."

Then he realized what he'd said, blushed purple, and everyone laughed.

"Excuse me," Dr. Greenleaf said, tapping on the microphone to get everyone's attention. "There seems to be a slight problem. Could we please be seated? I need everyone to be seated for a few minutes, please. I'm very sorry."

The Martha Washington Academy team went back to their places. They held hands and whispered. The Judson Christian High team sat back down at their table. A large block of fear moved into Tim's stomach and sat there.

When they saw Miss Shore gesturing forcefully at a blue binder at the judges' table, they knew something bad was about to happen.

"We won the match! What is she doing?" asked Emma.

"I guess we didn't win her over at lunchtime," Lenny said. "She found a way to make us lose."

Andrea began to cry in earnest. Tim took her hand.

"Let's be glad we got this far," Arthur said earnestly. "If she had been our sponsor like she wanted to be, we would have quit months ago. Let's be thankful for what we have. Second place is fantastic. Miss Thistle will be happy with a second place trophy to put in the case."

Dr. Greenleaf conferred with the judges, then turned to speak with the obviously agitated Mrs. Lemon. After a few moments, Mrs. Lemon rushed out of the room.

Dr. Greenleaf spoke into the microphone again. "There is a rules question. We wish, of course, that rules questions could all be solved prior to the final match—" here he glared at Miss Shore—"but that isn't always done. So here we are. Rule forty-seven clearly states that an official sponsor listed on the Team Registration form be in attendance for the team to compete. A party present insists that Judson Christian High fails on this count. If this proves to be the case, Judson will forfeit and Martha Washington will win. Please stand by while we sort it out."

Dr. Greenleaf told a few jokes at which everyone laughed nervously while he stalled; no one was quite sure why.

Then Mrs. Lemon came rushing back in. She waved a sky-blue sheet of paper. "Here it is," she shouted.

"Thank you," said Dr. Greenleaf. "This is the official competition registration sent in by Judson Christian High in January. It lists the main sponsor as Miss M. Thistle. Is she here?" He paused. A wistful look passed over his face. "I used to know a Miss M. Thistle myself, years ago." He paused and turned sharply to the Judson Christian team. "Did Judson Christian used to be called Adoniram Judson High?

Tim stood, "Yes, sir. Same school, same Miss Maggie Thistle that you know, sir! But no, she's not here. She's in the hospital."

"Maggie Thistle," Dr. Greenleaf said. "Little black woman, about this high, about my age?" His voice boomed.

"Yes, sir. She hoped you would remember her."

"Remember her? She made me!"

Miss Shore spoke up, "The point is, she isn't here, so Judson doesn't win."

"Not so fast," said Dr. Greenleaf. "There's another name listed here, a Dr. W. Ross. Is Dr. Ross present in the auditorium?"

"No, sir," said Tim, dropping his head. "Dr. Ross went with her in the ambulance."

Miss Shore grinned and swayed to some inner music.

"Okay, two down. There's one more name listed. Is there a Miss B. Shore present?"

The team gasped.

Miss Shore gasped. "Me? My name is on that?"

Dr. Greenleaf thundered, "You are Miss B. Shore?"

She nodded.

"And you're obviously here." He stared hard at her. She sank into a chair, limp as a rag doll.

"Judson wins," he said again.

The large runner-up trophy was given to the Martha Washington team. They carried it off to cheers and yelled, "We're going to Disney World!"

Then an even larger trophy was presented. Tim accepted it for the team. Pictures were taken, hugs were exchanged, and tears were wiped off joyous faces.

"Now," said Dr. Greenleaf, interrupting the general riot of emotion between the Judson team and their parents. "Let's get this trophy to Miss Thistle!"

"Let's, as in *let us* as in *you and us*?" asked Arthur.

"Generally that is what *let's* means," said Dr. Greenleaf.

"We came in our school van," said Mr. Barnaby. "It's a five-hour drive."

"So it is," said Dr. Greenleaf. "So what we'll do is this. All parents will go home how they came. The team and I will go in the university jet." He grinned. "If that's all right with everyone, that is."

"I've decided I will attend college next year," Arthur announced suddenly, motivated as he was to have a jet at his disposal.

"Miss Thistle gave you a choice?" said Dr. Greenleaf. "She must be slacking off."

Miss Shore sat in the back row of the auditorium alone. Mrs. Barnaby walked over and sat beside her.

"You're here to mock me," said Miss Shore.

"No. I know how life hurts sometimes. "

"I guess I haven't been thinking about anyone else's problems for a long time." said Bethany. She blew her nose. "I've been too busy hating God for the difficulties in my life. I let that spill over onto hating those kids who never did anything wrong to me."

Mrs. Barnaby hugged her. "Don't worry. It's okay. No one ever hated you back."

Miss Shore blew her nose. "I'm so embarrassed. I behaved so badly."

The two women sat in silence for several minutes. At last Miss Shore said, "I was so angry that Miss Thistle got to do the team instead of me. I had no idea Dr. Hamilton had decided to include me. I never gave him a chance to tell me."

She tucked her long hair behind her ears and looked out over the now-empty auditorium.

"You know, I saw that blue paper. It was lying on Dr. Hamilton's desk that day I quit. He was trying to get me to take some time off to think. I thought it was a notice that I was being fired, so I quit."

She looked up at Mrs. Barnaby. "I was so wrong about everything."

"It's okay," Mrs. Barnaby said, hugging her. "Ever since Eden, God's been in the business of reconciliation."

"You believe that, the snake and the apple?" asked Miss Shore.

"The snake, the fruit, the promise of the Savior. Every word," said Mrs.Barnaby.

"Tell me more," said Miss Shore.

Chapter 26

Miss Thistle stirred. She tried to open her eyes, then gave up. She had been sleeping so long! She felt so groggy! Was she in a hospital? She vaguely remembered having seen the Rosses earlier, but she couldn't be sure. Had Dr. and Mrs. Hamilton stopped by with flowers, or was that a dream? There did seem to be the scent of roses in the room.

She was alone. The visitors must have left when she was sleeping so soundly. *Why am I here anyway? Wasn't there something important I was supposed to be doing today?*

Radiation. I'm having radiation therapy. No, that's tomorrow after the Superbrain finals.

Then the realization: *I missed the finals. I missed seeing Thaddeus.*

She remembered it all again. The early morning gathering at the Barnabys. That overwhelming feeling of weakness. The fall.

"Dear Lord," she prayed. "I wanted to be there so badly." She wondered frantically how the team had done.

There was a knock at the door, and the Superbrain team crept in. Arthur carried a bouquet of daisies.

Miss Thistle opened her eyes. "Oh," she said. "You're here." She searched the wall for the clock, saw it was only five-thirty, and realized the team must not have gone to the finals after all. They could never have returned so soon otherwise. It was such a long drive.

"You didn't go," she said flatly.

"We did go," said Andrea smiling. She took the flowers from Arthur and put them on Miss Thistle's bedside table beside Dr. Hamilton's roses.

"You're back early," she said sadly.

"We flew," said Tim.

Tim grinned. Arthur grinned. Lenny grinned. Andrea grinned. Emma grinned.

Miss Thistle stared back at them, saying nothing, but with wide open, questioning eyes.

"Here," said Andrea, "Let me adjust your bed so you're sitting up. We have something to show you."

"What is it?" asked Miss Thistle, "Tell me!"

"It's the State Championship Superbrains trophy!" boomed a deep voice. The kids moved aside while Dr. Greenleaf carried the trophy to Miss Thistle's bedside and held it for her to touch.

Miss Thistle did not even see the trophy. She saw only the face of Thaddeus Greenleaf.

"Thaddeus," said Miss Thistle.

"Hello, Miss Thistle," he said, smiling down on her. "Long time."

"Sorry about that note. It was awful."

"Indeed it was." Dr. Greenleaf pulled out his wallet. He turned toward the kids, winked at them, and unfolded a yellowed sheet of paper from his wallet. He read: "Dear Thaddeus, Since you're not going to college, I'm no longer going with you. You could've been something, but you're determined to be a nobody. I'm sure I'll always love you, but don't come back here without an education. Shame on you. Maggie Thistle."

"Oh dear," said Miss Thistle. "That was harsh."

"It was a kick in the pants! Just what I needed," he said. He turned to the kids and said, "I think Miss Thistle will agree that I have an education now, so maybe she'll speak to me again. If you don't mind, there's a little matter of forty years to catch up on."

The Superbrain champions smiled and snuck quietly out the door.

Miss Thistle and Thaddeus Greenleaf talked for hours.

"I told the children this morning I knew this was going to be the happiest day of my life," Miss Thistle said. "And I believe it has been."

Dr. Greenleaf leaned over and kissed her on the forehead. "Get well, Maggie," he said. "You have no idea how much you're still needed in this world."

Phone calls, text messages, and e-mails had flashed through the air all day. By the time the Superbrains arrived at Max's Pizza Palace, the place was ablaze in the purple and gold of Judson Christian High School. The JCHS Patriot pep band blasted pep songs while everyone cheered and sang. Jenny and her fellow cheerleaders led the mob in rousing Judson Christian High cheers.

Pizza and soda pop were consumed in vast quantities. Mr. Max, owner of the pizza palace, himself arrived to see what the hullabaloo was about. Upon realizing what a publicity bonanza this was for him, he called the television station and the newspaper.

By the time the party was over, the Superbrains were bona fide celebrities with their joyous faces and get-well messages of love to Miss Thistle plastered across the local media outlets.

The headline in the *Ledger* the next morning blazed: JUDSON CHRISTIAN HIGH SUPERBRAINS EMERGE VICTORIOUS.

Mr. Barnaby hugged Tim and shouted, "You blasted them to the moon!"

In their little brick home on Maple Street, Dr. Ross kissed his wife.

In the hospital, Miss Thistle greeted Dr. Jones and smiled. "Shall we get started on those treatment modalities of yours?" she said. "I think I'll try living."